To Vickie 63 Ranch 2012

Cowgirl's Justice

The Rancher Series

Cowgirl's Justice

Dawn Nelson

Gray Dog Press

Published by

Gray Dog Press
Spokane, Washington
www.GrayDogPress.com

Cowgirl's Justice

ISBN-13: 978-1-936178-03-2

Layout & Design by Russel Davis
Cover Photo by Claudine K. Angstrom

Printed in the U.S.A.

Every good cowboy or cowgirl is only
granted one good dog and one great horse
a lifetime, and now a good dog I must find.

—An unknown cowboy

Chapter 1

The little town of Danville, Washington, was unusually hot for a mid-May morning as Jesse Walker turned her truck and horse trailer down Main Street, heading straight for the general store.

Things hadn't changed much in the last ten years, but the sidewalks were sagging just a little more than she remembered. The old buildings looked pretty much the same. She noticed a few new signs and stores she didn't remember but for the most part Danville hadn't changed all that much from the outside looking in.

She had to admit Danville had grown a little, but it still had the air of the little old town she remembered from her childhood. With her window rolled down she could smell the old wood of the buildings that lined Main Street and the numerous fir and pine trees that skirted the town and made Danville home.

She realized little had changed but her. Her long dark hair still hung in a braid down her back just like before she had left so many years ago, but now a few gray hairs scattered here and there marked the passing of time.

Her green eyes, hidden behind her dark sunglasses, had a few more lines around them and had lost a lot of their childhood twinkle. The life of a rodeo star was hard and the life as the wife of one was harder. She had never planned on ever coming back to this town again, but after coming home and finding another woman in her husband's arms, she had nowhere else to go but back home to her parents' ranch.Her parents had both died ten years earlier in a car wreck and had left the ranch to her, but she had never come back after the funeral. It held too many memories and would be a little too painful to come back to. She had known that even then.

She had no clue what kind of shape the old homestead was in, even though she had sent money every month to keep the place in shape. It was being seen after by a caretaker, Logan Wilson. Logan and his wife Mary lived in the old bunkhouse on the ranch.

Logan had been her father's right-hand man around the ranch before he died. She remembered Logan as being old even back then; she couldn't imagine how old he must look now. Ten years was a long time, but then maybe she was the only one who had aged.

Danville had always been a mystical place for her. Her memories were always of a town that contained her childhood, wild and free with no worries and no rules.

Jesse wished she had taken the time to call ahead and tell Logan and Mary that she was coming, but as soon as she'd found the whore in her bed all she could do was grab the essentials and hook up the trailer before she left. She managed to get her stallion, Boe, and her barrel-racing gelding, Cozy. She loaded as many of her broodmares as she could fit in her twenty-four-foot trailer.

She managed to get seven of them loaded but figured she could send Marnie, her best friend, after the other three and assumed Marnie could bring them up to her at the ranch some day. Marnie was one lady Jesse knew who was in desperate need of a vacation. Maybe Danville would be a good change of scenery for the both of them.

She had known Marnie long before she ever met Hank. Marnie and Jesse had met at a 4-H camp in Idaho when she was about fifteen and they had instantly become friends. Marnie was quiet and polite while Jesse was the exact opposite.

Marnie had actually warned her away from Hank when she first met him, but Jesse didn't listen. She never listened. Who was she kidding?

She should have known better than to marry a rodeo cowboy, at least that much was apparent to her now. She was seventeen when she had met Hank. They were married right after her parents died. The next spring, in fact, when she turned eighteen.

They eloped to Vegas. She had wanted a real wedding—white dress, dancing, the whole shebang—but Hank said eloping was the only way he would marry her as he did not like the idea of a big show. She should have turned around and run right then, but she didn't. Hank not liking a big show was a joke; after all, he loved the limelight of the rodeo arena.

"Hindsight is always twenty-twenty," muttered Jesse. She found herself laughing at her outburst.

Hank was almost twenty years older than she was. He was thirty-seven when they married. But he was a star bull rider and she was a nobody when they married and pretty much still was even though she was a star barrel racer in her own right.

Now, she was just known as "Hank's wife," but never by his last name. It was the only smart thing she did, keeping her own last name, Walker.

Montgomery was not a bad last name, but Jessica Montgomery did not sound that good to her back then and now the idea of that name made her cringe.

"Thank God I was smart about that at least," Jesse said. "If anybody sees me talking to myself they'll think I'm touched in the head for sure. Maybe I'm touched in the head for coming back here after all this time."

Monthly updates and letters were all that she had to prove that her ranch was still there. Six thousand acres, a big house, numerous outbuildings, fifty head of cattle, and who knew what else had been acquired over the years.

Jesse didn't know what kind of shape the refrigerator or cupboards were in so she figured she better stop at the general store and pick up a few things. Some cleaning supplies probably would not hurt either. Ten years of dust and dirt might need a broom and some bleach. More than likely Logan and Mary had kept the basics up with the house, but cleaning would help Jesse ease the stress she was feeling at this moment.

Jesse figured she was coming home to a ghost town. No mining or timber should have cut down the number of people in town, but instead she noticed it seemed to have doubled or even tripled in size.

The protesters had shut down the mines, and shortly afterward the major logging companies were run out of the woods, too. She knew that there probably weren't that many jobs available in the area, but she would worry about finding work when her money began to run out.

In her pocket was two thousand dollars. She knew the cattle and the ranch should be able to support her but it was going to be a while before she could hire someone to help her learn more about breeding and to help Logan. After all he was getting older and if she began to build the ranch up again he would need help.

People bustled in and out of stores, trying to keep cool in the blistering heat, women in sundresses and men in shorts and ponytails. The town had changed, Jesse thought as she read some of the store signs. "Herbs For Sale," read one sign; another showed "No Mining Or Killing Of Our Trees," and yet another in front of the old saloon read, "No Drinking Allowed."

"Ha, I don't believe it!" Jesse said. "Danville a dry town? From seven saloons to zero in just twenty years." Jesse was shocked at all the changes that had occurred in Danville. It looked like the same from the outside but it seemed to be filled with foreign beings that resembled people but looked like hippies.

As Jesse pulled up in front of the general store, she noticed a few changes there as well. When she was a kid, an old chair used to sit on the porch. In that chair every day Old Tom sat telling stories of the olden days.

He had been replaced with a sign, which read, "No Loitering." His chair was nowhere to be found. That fact was a little painful to Jesse, as she had always enjoyed Tom's stories, especially the ones about cowboys and Indians. Tom was a part of this town just as the seven saloons had been; a lot of stories were lost with Tom gone.

The full heat hit her as she stepped from her pickup. Sweat beaded on her forehead.

"Ugh. It's hot out here," she muttered.

The steps made the same squeaking noise she remembered from her childhood, protesting against another day's use. As she stepped inside the cool store, she realized that was the only thing that remained the same. Hell and damnation, whoever invaded this town had done a good job of it.

The walls that used to be lined with shovels and picks now held a display of clothing in earthy tones. The old display of candy had been replaced by packages of nuts and dried fruit. Oat bars and ryegrass wafers took the place of Milky Way and Snickers.

Nothing looked the same but the ceiling. It was going to be hard to live in this town again. Jesse was hoping that maybe a plague would come and infect everybody who wore earth tones and smelled of dandelion leaves or buttermilk cologne.

"Excuse me, may I help you?" A short bald man came out of the back room and interrupted her thoughts.

"Maybe. Where are the Wilsons who used to own this store?" Jesse remembered the Wilsons had always been so nice and usually did their best to carry anything you might want or need. "Do they still own it?"

"Oh gosh no, they moved a long time ago. Eight years at least I would say. Did you know them?" the balding man asked. Jesse didn't like him and didn't know quite why. She had never liked change, but this man looked a little like a rat with his beady little eyes looking out from behind a pair of broad-rimmed, thick-lensed glasses.

"No, I just needed some supplies and it doesn't look like you carry them. Is there anywhere in town that might have grain and regular grocery items?" Jesse asked, fearing the response.

"Regular grocery items? What is it that you think I carry?" The man's blood boiled at the question. Jesse watched as red crept up his neck and soon his whole face looked red. Jesse hadn't meant to offend him.

"I need whole milk from a cow, cleaning supplies, candy, chocolate, those kind of things."

"Milk from a cow? Goat milk is much better for you, and that's right over there." He pointed to a cooler along the wall at the end of the store.

"Yes, it probably is, but I don't like goats. Is there a place that sells chocolate, cow's milk, cleaning supplies, and that kind of stuff?"

"Yes, the Walker Grocery store at the end of the street has all that kind of stuff, even real cow's milk," the balding man replied stiffly as he fiddled with some bags of stuff on the counter. Cornballs and alga crisps, yuck. Jesse wondered if he actually ever sold anything.

"Where would that be located? Wait a minute, you said the Walker grocery store?" Aside from her parents Jesse had been the only other Walker in town. She guessed it could have been someone who moved in with the same last name, but didn't think it was possible. It was a southern name, and Danville was far from the South.

"Yes, Walker, it's owned by, oh gosh, what is her name… it will come to me, hold on. Bert and Martha Walker… their daughter, I can't think of her name. I want to say Tessa but I know that's not right." He scratched his head as Jesse winced in financial pain.

"Jessica Walker?" Jesse questioned through clenched teeth.

"Yes, that does sound right. Anyway the store is just down the street—two blocks, hang a left. It's what used to be the old mill." The balding man watched with his beady little eyes narrowing even more as Jesse marched from the store, anger evident in every stride she took.

Who the hell had bought a store in her name? Is this where her money had been going every month, to keep the place up and stocked? She was going to get to the bottom of this and right away. That no-good caretaker had spent her money on a store instead of her place. When she found him she was going to string him up by his toenails and spit in his eye. If he was lucky that was all she would do to him.

What the heck was Logan doing? Had his brains aged way past thinking? She thought she knew Logan pretty well; just goes to show that you can never really know anyone. This might just put a bump in her and Logan's friendship.

The heat outside suddenly didn't seem like much compared to the heat around her collar. She jumped in her pickup, drove down two blocks, and turned left. The Old Mill had been a dump when she left. Why the hell someone would spend money on that place was beyond her. It would take a fortune to fix it up, and she'd be dammed if she was going to sink any money into that old fallen-down junk of a building.

As she rounded the corner the mill loomed up ahead. Holy cow. Someone had put a lot of work and money into the place. It looked great; new paint and boards on the sidewalk, a huge sign reading "Walker's Grocery & Feed Store," and it had a horse and rider turning a barrel. She pulled the pickup to a stop at the curb and stared in awe. The place looked great.

She grabbed her purse and strode in through the two swinging doors. The place smelled great of feed and leather. She looked around at all the bags of feed and horse tack; someone had done a lot of work to this place. One whole side of the store had four or five aisles of food—real food—cereal, soup, chili, bread, and cleaning supplies. She watched as four ladies with shopping carts filled with food and tack ambled from aisle to aisle. What a great idea! Tack, feed, and groceries all in one place.

She walked over to the tack and pulled a bridle off the rack, running it over her fingers and looking very closely at the bridle. She realized somebody knew their tack. It was good quality, not made in Japan or China. A large picture on the wall brought back all her furies: a life-size copy of her on Cozy turning a barrel.

"Damn," Jesse muttered. "What the hell was Logan thinking when he did all this?"

"May I help you?" A woman's soft voice cut through her fog of anger. She was a rather pretty lady, and Jesse guessed her to be around forty years old. She stood about five ten and had a tough, no-nonsense demeanor about her.

"Yes, I hope so. Who is the manager of this place?" Jesse realized the woman was staring at her and that damn cutout behind her.

"Logan is, but I'm sure you already know that, Jessica, or is it Jess?" The woman stood straight as an arrow and looked right through Jesse. Jesse took a good long look at the lady before her.

Her backbone was straight and Jesse guessed it had gotten that way from many an argument won and not backed away from. A woman like that, Jesse knew, was one to be idolized and for some reason she looked very familiar. She was as tough as saddle leather. Her face was tan from working out in the sun all day, Jesse guessed; her hands didn't look soft, but calloused and used to a full day's work.

"Jesse or Jess works. What's your name?" Jesse questioned. Nobody ever called her by Jessica unless she was in trouble. Logan always called her Jessica no matter how many times she would correct him or ask him to call her Jess or Jesse.

"Molly Tillson. I was a good friend of your mother's; you might not remember me, that was ten years ago." Oh, of course, how could Jesse have forgotten Molly? She was a good woman to know if you got into a sticky spot, that's what her mother had always said. A crack shot with a rifle, too, she remembered.

"I remember you, Molly. Tell me something, who signs your monthly checks?" Curiosity was eating away at Jesse; she wanted to know who was paying for all of this.

"Logan does, but he isn't here right now, he's up at the homestead. Said you had a mare foaling and he needed to get home to check on her."

Jesse knew now he was up to no good. They never had any broodmares on the place. He was buying useless things that the ranch didn't need, just spending her money. Well, she was going to put an end to that, however she did have to admit the store definitely showed the potential of helping her out financially. Maybe she wouldn't have to look for work after all.

"Logan might be back soon. Would you like to wait here?" Molly asked. "I'm sure you would like to see the books."

"What books?" she asked, and then realized she was talking about the financial books. "Oh, yes, that might be good. I guess I had better look at them." Jesse wanted to know how bad this place was doing. Besides, when she told Logan to go to hell she wanted something to back it up with. "Tell me, where is Logan staying?"

"He bought the old Lawson place next to your spread, that way I guess he's never far from home. He might still be staying in the bunkhouse. Or maybe Justin bought the place, I'm not sure," Molly stated.

"The old Lawson place is huge, how could he afford that? Does he work somewhere else as well?" Now Logan had bought another ranch with her money. Jesse did not like Logan right now. "And Justin, who is he?"

"Justin is Logan's grandson. I believe you know me better than that. I hate sticking my nose where it doesn't belong. I don't know how he affords anything, I'm sure it's legal, and he hasn't made the old place look half bad," Molly commented as a customer walked in the store. A young woman and her teenage girl headed straight to the horse tack. Molly left Jesse's side and strolled over to assist them. Jesse watched as the young girl picked out a bridle and turned to look at her mother for approval.

Molly smiled as the mother nodded her head. Jesse watched as Molly lowered her head to the girl's ear and whispered something. The girl's head whirled around to face Jesse, and she headed Jesse's way.

"Are you really Jesse Walker?" The girl's smile was enough to make Jesse feel as if her life wasn't half bad.

"Yes I am. What can I do for you?" Jesse asked.

"My name is Kelly. We live just down the road from your place. I do a little bit of barrel racing. I idolize you—when I grow up I want to be a barrel racer just like you. Would you sign my bridle? My mom and I shop here all the time just because you own the store. Where's Cozy?"

Jesse didn't know what to say. Since she had married Hank she had been so busy following him around the rodeo circuit she never realized she had any fans of her own. "Cozy is out in the trailer in front of the store. He's the second horse in there if you would like to pet him."

"Really? Oh my gosh, nobody is going to believe this at school. I'll be right back, Mom." With that, Kelly was out the door.

"Thank you, she has always been a huge fan of yours. I heard about your breakup with Hank. I'm sorry," her mother said.

"Wow, they're already talking about my breakup with Hank. It's only been a day; I guess news travels fast," Jesse said. She couldn't believe it. She hoped they made Hank and that whore out to be horrible people. She hoped the next bull Hank got on would send him straight to hell.

"You forget this is a small town," Molly was quick to put in.

"Yes, well if you will excuse me I have some work to do." She quickly signed the bridle and Molly pointed her toward the back room to look at the financial books for the store. Jesse spent about twenty minutes with her nose in the books before she realized that the store was grossing about one hundred thousand a year.

"Not bad. Well, I've delayed it long enough, I had better get home and see what tornado has hit the house," Jesse muttered.

She bought a few cleaning supplies and other things of necessity from her own store and headed home. *Her own store.* that sounded pretty good, even though when she got hold of Logan she was going to have to make it a little miserable on him for doing all this without her approval.

Chapter 2

The old homestead was about five and a half miles from town, but the drive and her nerves made it seem more like five hundred. She feared what she might find. She knew it was a lot of work for an old man but somehow Logan had managed to get the store going good. She was still surprised and pleased at the amount of money it was bringing in.

She knew Logan had the help of Molly, but from what she remembered Logan was around sixty when she left; he had to be seventy or older by now. She couldn't imagine his grandson was that much help. He couldn't be that old, maybe eighteen or so. Even if he was a handyman, how much work could one kid and one old man get done?

She turned in the driveway, which housed a new sign that read "Walker Ranch The Running W." Wow, there had been a lot of changes around here. The driveway was smoother than she remembered it, and seemed longer, too. As she rounded the knoll, she lost her breath. The barns, outbuildings, and house all had new roofs and a fresh coat of paint. New corrals stretched out behind the barns, a new shed had been built, and runs for horses ran off the sides of it.

New trees had been planted. Flowers were growing out of flowerbeds she didn't remember. The whole place looked fresh and clean.

No activity could be seen anywhere, then suddenly out of the new building stepped an old man. She knew him instantly—it was Logan. He was tall for an elderly man, a little bent from the years of hard work but still recognizable to Jesse. Jesse knew that below that old gray felt cowboy hat that had definitely seen better days sat a nest of hair just as gray, maybe even white now.

As quick as he had exited, he scooped up a bucket of water from a nearby trough and disappeared back inside the building. She stepped out of her truck and followed him into the building. She could hear voices coming from the last stall. She wondered who could be helping Logan out there. Maybe that was Justin, his grandson, or maybe Logan's wife Mary?

Logan had stepped back inside the stall. The mare they called Maggie had just delivered her baby and was eagerly nuzzling the young stud colt, trying to get him to stand on his feet for the first time. Logan had just fetched clean water for Maggie to drink and then he handed the bucket to Justin.

Justin had been helping around there since his mother passed away nine and a half years before. Justin had nowhere else to go and was fresh out of the army. Recently out of a dead-end relationship, the thought of relaxing and working with his Grandpa Logan sounded like a good life. When he showed up on the ranch his grandpa was relieved to have him. The work was getting too much for one guy and the old ranch was getting pretty worn out.

The Walkers, his grandpa had said, were good and honest folk who had been killed when a drunken tractor-trailer driver swerved and hit their truck, taking himself and them over a cliff. They had left everything to their daughter Jessica Walker, who Logan had told him was trying to follow the rodeo circuit after her husband, who was supposedly some big bull rider. Justin had never followed the rodeo circuit and didn't have time for it now.

May meant cows to brand and turn out, mares to foal out, and fences to fix. The Walkers, he was told, had run into bad times, and had been barely making it. When he showed up the place had been pretty run down; the old house and barns were ramshackle to say the least. After a few boards and a few coats of paint he had them looking better. He had planted flowers and trees to make the place feel more like a home.

He jumped right into learning about cattle, bloodlines, and EPDs, and how to read charts and graphs, how to tell one cow from another. He came up with a few shortcuts himself. He planted some of the fields with alfalfa and raised hay off of them to lower the production cost. He irrigated the meadows to make the pasture last longer and in doing so it added a hundred or more pounds to the calves' weaning weight in the fall. He learned about quarter horse bloodlines and bought a top quality stallion and a few broodmares for himself. With the fillies out of his mares, he built a herd for the Running W, and he found a nice stallion and bought it to cover them.

The ranch now had about sixty head of broodmares and four hundred head of cattle, and not just any cattle—it had registered Black Angus cattle. With the money from all the crops he bought the mill and opened it up as a feed store, which took some relief off the Running W during tax time.

"Hey Justin, you daydreaming?" Logan's old voice interrupted his thoughts.

"A little, I was just thinking about all we've done around here," Justin explained.

"Yes, we have gotten a lot done, the place looks good. But I think there's still more to do, so if you get done daydreaming about that there stud colt and all his future accomplishments we can go get the fence fixed up on the north range," Logan added.

Justin knew Logan was upset about something today; he wasn't himself. He normally would have been just as eager as

Justin to wonder at what the colt would become, or be just as happy to stand here and watch him stand and nurse for the first time. Something was off in Logan's demeanor.

"What's wrong with you today, Grandpa Logan?" Justin questioned.

"Nothing, I just need to get some other things done and with you standing around we aren't getting anything accomplished," Logan barked.

He didn't want or mean to be so nasty but with Molly's call a few minutes ago, he knew Jessica was on her way home and he wanted the place to look perfect for her. He had no clue what kind of a person she had grown into. Molly also mentioned that Jessica was having some kind of problem with Hank, or so the rumor mill went. Logan had never liked Hank from the first time he met him. Cruel and cranky with a huge chip on his shoulder and an extremely large ego was a description that you would be able to pick Hank out of a crowd with.

Logan knew he should tell Justin that Jessica was coming home. The truth was he didn't know why he wasn't telling him. He knew Justin had been through a hard breakup with Annie while he was in the army. Justin would never talk about it, but in the last nine years Logan had watched Justin turn around and steer clear of all women but his grandmother.

Logan found one woman in particular, Karla Jenson, quite pretty and young. She was head over heels for Justin. Logan hoped deep down inside that Justin would fall for Karla and settle down, but it didn't seem like that was the plan for them. Justin declined every offer Karla would make to go riding or out to dinner or dancing it didn't seem to matter. Logan feared if he told Justin that Jessica was coming home, he would turn tail and run like a wounded rabbit.

"Okay, Grandpa, I'm ready to go work on the fence if you are," Justin stated as he stood up straight and followed Logan out of the stall. He turned and latched the door to Maggie's stall when a figure caught the corner of his eye. He turned and saw a slender, rather tall woman walking down the breezeway. She looked all business, like someone who worked for the Secret Service or something; her stride was long and purposeful.

Jesse almost stumbled as she watched a broad-chested man step from the box stall behind Logan. His good looks were almost hidden behind a couple days growth of his beard, but they were definitely still there. He was tall and tan from days of sunlight soaking into his skin. His hair was dark, almost black as his hand ran through it before placing a tattered black cowboy hat back upon his head.

She remembered Hank's saying, *Good guys wear black hats, gray is for old cowboys and women, and only assholes wear white.* Hank wore a black hat but she knew white was really his color.

She suddenly realized she was staring and quickly turned to Logan.

"Logan, hello, how are you doing?" She hugged his neck and stepped back. "I'm Jessica, don't you remember me? I'm sorry I didn't call before, I just didn't have any time." She knew that was a lie but it sounded like a good reason not to call.

"Jessica! Hi dear," Logan's voice quaked. "You're just like I remembered you, pretty as ever."

"Thank you, Logan, and you don't look a day over thirty yourself," Jesse teased.

Logan's eyes twinkled as he laughed. "Ah, do go on. I like to hear pretty girls flirt with me. Oh, I almost forgot, Jessica girl, this here is my grandson Justin, he's been helping me out. He bought the Lawsons' old homestead next door and has been fixing it up. He's quite a handyman."

"Hello, and congratulations on your purchase of the Lawson place." Jesse was somehow expecting Logan's grandson to be five, not a grown man. Well at least that cleared up the Lawson place, now if only she could clear up the purchase of the store. She would talk to Logan later about the store. Now, it was time for hellos, not yelling.

She also wanted to know how this man could have afforded the Lawson place. It was big and most likely came stocked with whatever animals the Lawsons had had at the time of sale. She guessed it would have cost him close to one million dollars to buy it.

"Thank you," Justin said before turning to Logan. "I'd better go fix that fence up in the north range, before we lose the cows into the Forest Service land and have to go chase them down for the next two weeks."

Justin knew he was looking for a way to get away from talking to Jessica any more. Annie, his last girlfriend, had taught him all he needed to know about women—they were cruel and heartless. Kind and warmhearted when you first met them and of course in public, then there was the other side, cruel and cunning like a rattlesnake stalking a mouse.

Annie had been such a sweet and caring woman until he got a little money and then suddenly she wanted all the money and none of him. They had planned to get married but when he gave her an engagement ring she threw it back at him and told him he could afford a better one.

"What would my friends say if they saw me wearing a one-carat diamond engagement ring when they know you can afford a bigger one?" she cooed afterward. When he informed her it was just the engagement ring, not the wedding ring, she flew into a fury of flying fists.

"If you truly loved me you would buy me a bigger one," she informed him again after he had calmed her down.

"Yes Annie, but if you really loved me, that one would be just fine." With that he turned and left her standing there with her mouth agape like a bird awaiting a fly.

From that day on, he had sworn off commitment-minded females or telling anyone that he had money. He dealt better with animals than women any day. To this day, he had never had a cow or horse tell him they didn't like him because he could afford better hay than he was giving them.

"Yeah, I guess you had better go fix it. I'll show Jessica the house and all the improvements we made around here. I wanted to help her clean up the house anyway before nightfall," Logan put in. Justin excused himself and strode outside to his pickup. A day on the fence line was just what he needed. A pretty woman was trouble in every aspect of the word, and Jessica was definitely pretty.

Justin knew in the long run he was working for a woman, but without her around it felt like he was just working for himself. But now with her being back it was going to be hard to evade her totally. He knew that, but he would have to deal with that later.

Jessica was glad to be alone with Logan but she couldn't help but watch Justin leave; his narrow waist and long legs drew her breath away. He was a beautiful man but a little shy for her taste, but then she was still a married woman for a few more weeks until she could file for a divorce and get rid of Hank forever.

She had no clue what a divorce entailed. She had never planned on ever getting one until she saw that woman in Hank's arms. That sight would never leave her mind, ever. The part that bothered her most was when she ran from the room and Hank didn't even come out of the house or try to stop her. He just laid there almost as if she had annoyed him by the sudden interruption. He had probably gone back to what he was doing after she left.

She almost wished she had grabbed a gun and shot him, or at least at him enough to make him jump out of bed. Yes, Hank was a big rodeo star, but he had two very annoying diseases: women, and being lazy. Jesse had hated the fact that he had never wanted to work on their own place or ride their own horses, and he could never even lift a hand to do dishes or water the dog.

She knew Hank only wanted her for her parents' ranch, but when they died, she told him they sold it. It outraged him to no end that she hadn't been left the ranch. He said they should buy it. She hadn't wanted to move back home and live on the ranch at that time. A lie was easier than moving back and she just never took the time to change it to the truth. It's amazing how a little lie grows and grows until the truth is no longer recognizable.

After a few years, he stopped bugging her about buying the ranch back and went on a drinking spree. Jesse couldn't figure out why he had wanted the Running W so badly, but now it didn't matter. He was out of her life for good and the ranch was hers.

After her truck was unloaded of the groceries and cleaning supplies, the broodmares were turned loose in a vacant pasture beside the house. Boe and Cozy were stalled for the night in two empty stalls she had found in the new barn. Logan and Jessica went to giving the house a whole cleaning. The dust wasn't as bad as she thought it would be. Logan explained that about once a month Mary would clean up the house and wash all the windows.

It didn't take as long as she thought it would, and soon she and Logan were sitting at the table drinking a cup of coffee talking about old times and changing times. The conversation was mild for the most part but each knew they were skipping around one big subject.

"Logan, whose idea was it to buy the store?" Jesse blurted out as she took a gulp of coffee that burned all the way down; she wished she had taken a smaller sip. She had to know why it was purchased and who was paying for it. "I have to know who is paying the bills. Because if it's me, I don't have that much money anymore. Hank saw to that in too many ways."

"I was wondering when you would ask. Justin bought it for tax purposes. After he made so many adjustments to the property we found the ranch was making too much money, so he said we needed a tax write-off. So the store was purchased and fixed up. He did most of the work himself. You're paying the bills in a sense but you'll never know it. Molly and Gus are our only two employees," Logan stated.

"I see. You know, I was pissed off when I first saw it, but now I guess I see it was for the ranch's own good." She knew what he was saying made sense.

"I figured you may have been a little mad when you saw the store. Molly said she showed you the books and she thought you seemed pleased by the look on your face afterwards."

"The store is doing well. I have to admit that much."

"The town needed it." Logan looked sad as he stated the fact.

"So what's happened to Danville? It looks the same but the people are a lot, how shall I say it, different. I guess that's the best word for the sentence." Jesse had to know what had happened to her old hometown, why everybody was so different than she remembered.

When she was a kid, the Old Mill had corrals behind it and that was where the monthly cattle sales were held in town, but there were no corrals or sale yards that she saw behind there now. It was almost as if cows had been exiled from town, and so had the normal everyday people.

Logan paused before he told her the story he knew he would have to tell her sometime. He had hoped to keep it from her awhile longer, but he guessed there was no time like the present. "About eight, eight and a half years ago, a big bus pulled into town. It was carrying about thirty people in all, all hippies, or 'earth people,' we called them. But they brought something new to town, something Danville had never seen in all its years." He paused for a moment and then continued. "Big money and drugs."

"They bought up the whole town, pretty much. Soon more buses rolled in and more drugs and more money. They tried to buy out the whole valley for their crops of marijuana but not everybody would sell, so they raised the food, grain, and fuel prices until regular folks could not afford anything around here. Everybody was being forced to sell out and leave town and find a new place to live.

"That's when we bought the mill. We tend to all the ranchers and other normal people's needs. They made it hard for us to make a start in the beginning but after a while they just left us alone and realized we weren't going anywhere. Lots of people died doing just what Justin is doing right now, running a fence line or checking a cow." Logan's eyes were grim as he looked out the window toward the north range. Jesse knew he was looking for Justin.

"So why were people dying? And why isn't the sheriff doing anything about them if they're growing drugs? Isn't that still illegal in these parts?" Jesse asked with just a hint of sarcasm.

"Well, what we called hippies were really a cult group. They were far worse than any hippie I've ever seen back in the seventies or eighties. The hippies, well they were all about herbs and peace, 'don't kill the trees' or 'don't mine,' that kind of stuff. A happy drug. That is what the hippies were into. They were against the war and fighting," Logan explained.

"So what was the cult group all about?" Jesse asked.

Logan looked out the window toward the north range again. Before he spoke Jesse could tell he was worried about Justin. She couldn't blame him. By the sounds of things she was starting to worry about him a little herself and she didn't even know the guy.

"They were after the whole town in a way. About three years ago all the killings started taking place. They butchered our cattle for the blood and organs, killed men and women for the same. But we couldn't prove anything, and poor old Sheriff Hoffman died trying to get evidence up on the east forty flats." Logan paused again and looked north.

He knew somewhere up there in the setting sun Justin was finishing his fence line, and he hoped it would be sooner rather than later. He worried something fierce when Mary or Justin would leave for the day and he had the job of sticking around the ranch waiting for their return.

"If you go riding around here you stick to your property and don't say anything to anyone. Basically, steer clear of strangers, Jessica," Logan instructed.

"So the new barn is nice, when did you guys build it?"

Jesse wanted to change the subject. She didn't like where this one was going or where she could tell Logan thought it would end. She knew she would have to address this issue later, but right now there was already too much new to worry about. What tomorrow might bring, it would bring, and she didn't need a corrupt town full of a blood-draining cult to worry her too.

"Oh, I guess it got built about four years ago now. Justin decided he wanted some broodmares and he wanted to start a herd for the ranch as well, so we built it for foaling and housing the stallions. Speaking of that, that is a nice stallion you brought. Where did you come up with him?" Jesse could tell Logan thought a lot of Justin's ideas and the way he planned ahead. She had started to think he had some pretty good ideas herself, but she wasn't going to tell him that until she knew him better.

"Boe is my stallion's name. He's been with me since Mom and Dad passed away," Jesse stated. Logan could see tears welling up in her eyes. "You see," she began, "Mom and Dad had a fifty–thousand-dollar insurance policy on each of them, so I went out and bought one of the nicest stud colts money could buy, and that was Boe."

What Jesse didn't tell Logan was that she used the money as soon as she got it, so that Hank couldn't or wouldn't get ahold of it and spend it on something for himself like a pickup or motorbike, entry fees, or whatever else he decided he wanted or needed at that time in his life.

Surprisingly she found herself relieved to be away from Hank. She didn't miss him or even feel like she wanted ever to see him again. Hank had never been a very nice guy, just a star bull rider. She guessed the life of a rodeo star seemed fun when she was younger. Now she just wanted to settle down and have her feet on solid ground, something Hank just couldn't figure out.

They sat for a while longer talking about nothing of importance until the coffee pot was empty. Jesse remembered she wanted to call Marnie and tell her to get the other three broodmares and haul them up to the ranch if she had the time.

Marnie was by far Jesse's closest friend. She was an opposite of Jesse through and through. Marnie was thirty and never married, very sweet and kind, and worked at the bank as a manager. She was quite successful and very beautiful; her shoulder-length blond hair was always perfectly groomed and never out of place. Unlike Jesse's, which had a mind of its own, much like its human host. She worked very hard at the bank with little gratitude and at numerous times Jesse had tried unsuccessfully to get her to quit the bank and work somewhere where she would be appreciated.

Getting up from the table she explained to Logan, "I have to call Marnie, one of my best friends back in Caldwell, and let her know that I've come up here and see if she would pick up three other mares I have down there."

Logan looked at her for a long time before he spoke. "I take it then we won't be seeing Hank around here."

Jesse smiled; even when she was a kid Logan always knew when she was not telling the whole story, and ten years hadn't changed a thing. She guessed you could know someone, if it was Logan, inside and out, since he never changed.

"I guess you could say that," Jesse muttered.

"Care to talk about it?" Logan asked. Logan knew Jesse was a person who never held things in for long without them eating away at her. She had to express her feelings outright or she would keep them bottled up to stew.

"Later, maybe." It was almost seven o'clock and she knew Marnie would be home. Jesse wanted to take care of her mares first; she was afraid of what Hank might do to them when he found her missing. She wouldn't put it past him to send them to market or give them away or something to that effect. "I want to get ahold of Marnie first."

Jesse picked up the receiver on the wall and dialed Marnie's number. It rang twice before she answered. Her sweet voice sounded concerned as she agreed to pick up the mares and asked about Jesse's well-being.

Logan listened to see if Jesse would tell her friend about the cult but it never came up, and he wondered why she would invite her friend up and not warn her about the danger. He figured maybe she didn't want to scare her only friend away.

Jesse and Marnie said their goodbyes and agreed upon Marnie driving up this weekend with the mares. With Logan's stories of the cult, Jesse knew she needed to tell Marnie something.

"Marnie, do me one favor. Come straight to the ranch, do not stop in town for anything at all. There are some strange people in town and Logan said they are dangerous, so please, when you cross the county line, do not stop for anyone or anything," Jesse added. She had decided not to tell her until she got here, but if something happened to Marnie, Jesse would never forgive herself.

"Are you sure you're safe there, Jess?" Marnie asked, deeply concerned. Jesse had always been so much stronger than her, Marnie knew that, but somehow she always felt like she had to protect Jesse from the outside world, much like a mother protects her child. Marnie had known Hank was a scoundrel. She just didn't know how to break it to Jesse that he was seen with a lot of different women.

She had warned Hank once that he had better stop seeing other women or she was going to tell Jesse. He told her if she wanted to break Jesse's heart to go ahead. Marnie knew it would hurt Jess, and in a way she was glad to find out that Jess saw it for herself and she hadn't had to break the news to her best friend.

"Yes, I think I'm pretty safe here. I have quite a bit of ground and I own a grocery and feed store. I think I'll be okay," Jesse assured her.

"Good. I'll be there Friday night around ten or so. I might end up coming Saturday morning since it will take me about ten hours to get there," Marnie replied. As she said goodbye to Jesse and looked around her cramped little apartment, she smiled.

"Like it or not, Jess, I'm moving up to help you out. I hate working with other people's money and now I'm going to go live on a cow ranch in the middle of nowhere." She smiled to herself. Marnie knew she wouldn't be much good out on the ranch, but she knew she could cook for the crew or at least work in Jesse's store until she figured out something else to do.

Logan and Jesse spent a few more hours sipping a new pot of coffee and talking about the ranch. Jesse was impressed with all the new things Justin and Logan had done to the place.

Logan sighed a sigh of relief when he saw the truck lights coming down the road behind the barn. Jesse watched as Justin stopped in front of the new barn. She almost laughed at the relief on Logan's face. The big softy, she thought. She watched as Justin stepped into the barn light and walked out of sight into the building. One thing she had to admit was that Justin was a good-looking man, even from a distance.

Logan stood and stretched. "Well, I had better get going and let you get some rest. Mary will be over tomorrow to help you get settled in and probably cook you breakfast."

"Tell her hello for me and I will see you in the morning." With that, he turned and left. Jesse watched his silhouette as he ambled toward the new barn. The place had changed so much with one man's help, but Logan was one man who she knew would never change. He was as steady as the mountains and she loved that about him.

He went with the flow but he made his own path. Jesse wished she could be more like him. She had always gone where Hank went and did things how he wanted them done. She hated feeling sorry for herself, but with the night in full force and her hating the loneliness that the night brought, it didn't seem too hard to feel sorry for all that she could have had or done with her life, but didn't.

She felt so old and alone sitting in front of the large window looking out into the darkness. She had been so carefree and young when she left this place over ten years ago. She was back now and going to make the most of her situation in life. Come what may she was going to take it in stride, she was going to live her life as if every moment was her last.

Jesse sat at the kitchen table for a few more minutes before she emptied her cup of coffee into the sink and headed up to her bedroom. She flopped down on her bed and laid back, loving the feeling of her bones and body relaxing.

"What a day, I'm so tired." The feather mattress molded to her body like a lover's arms and before she knew it, she was sound asleep and she hadn't even removed her boots.

Chapter 3

The singing of the robins outside her window made Jesse open her weary eyes, as did the annoying ring of the telephone by her bed. Who would be calling before breakfast? she asked herself as she wiped a little sleep from her eyes. It was hard to believe someone could wake up sleepier than when they went to bed.

"Holy cow! What time is it anyway?" Jesse mumbled as she fumbled for the clock and saw it was only 5:30. She picked up the receiver and cleared her throat.

"Hello." The voice on the line sounded quite familiar as it said hello back to her.

"Who is this?" asked Jesse, her mind still clouded from sleep.

"This is Jack, Jesse. Don't you remember me?" Jack who? Did she know a Jack?

"Jack who? How do I know you?" The only Jack she had ever known was Jack Smith from high school. They had been girlfriend and boyfriend until Hank came along.

"It's me, Jack Smith," he replied. "I heard you were back here in the big town of Danville and I had to call you and say hello. I know it's early but I wanted to know if you would meet me for lunch today around eleven thirty in town at Grandma's Café. It's still owned by Aunt Betty."

"Jack, I never thought you would still be in Danville after all this time. I thought you would be married and moved away," Jesse said as she sat up straight in bed. Maybe he was married. That would be ridiculous if a married man called his old girlfriend and invited her to lunch.

"I just couldn't leave. So, will you meet me, or not?" Jack questioned.

"Yes, I guess so. I will see you at eleven thirty at Grandma's." With that she hung up the phone. Jack had always been so sweet and caring. She hurt him bad, she knew, when she left without a word. She wondered if he still looked the same. He had always been a tall, gangly boy with blond hair and blue eyes. She knew she didn't look the same, so she figured he had most likely changed as well.

They had been boyfriend and girlfriend for about a year before Hank came along. They had never gotten serious. Jack had always wanted to, but she felt weird around him. Even then it was more of a brother-sister friendship than anything else. They pretty much just held hands, with an occasional kiss or two, but now maybe it would be different, maybe he would be different in a good way.

As she took a hot shower, Jesse was glad to feel the rest of the sleep washing away. She felt refreshed and ready for a new life, whatever it might bring. She dressed in her favorite pair of faded blue Wranglers and a black T-shirt. After pulling on her boots, she grabbed a gray sweater. Mornings could be a little cool up here so a light sweater seemed like a good idea.

As she headed to the barn to feed Cozy and Boe, the morning air was crisp but warming up fast. It was going to be another hot day. She hurried across the gravel driveway and into the barn. Cozy popped his head over his stall door and neighed his greeting. She kissed him on the muzzle.

"Good morning, gorgeous."

The horses were soon fed, and with Cozy and Boe watered she walked the aisles looking at the rest of the horses. A big gray gelding stood in one stall; his nameplate said, "Badger." He wasn't the friendliest horse by any means. He turned his butt to her and looked out the back window of his stall, as if to say she wasn't worth his time.

A big steel dust stallion occupied another stall—his nameplate read "To Catch a Reason." He was much happier to see Jesse as his nose nuzzled her cheek over the stall door. Jesse laughed and kissed him on the muzzle as well.

"Well aren't you a handsome boy?" she asked him as if expecting a reply.

He returned the affection with more nuzzling. Jesse spent some more time with him. She would definitely have to bring him a few treats sometime.

She stopped at the mare and foal's stall. The little stud colt was busy sucking and didn't realize he was being watched. The mare was busy eating some grain. Somebody was already up and out here this morning, probably Logan.

She unlatched the door, crept in, and sat down in the corner and waited for the colt to get done sucking before she petted him. He turned around after only a few minutes and walked right up to her. She held out her hand. He sniffed it and stuck his tongue out and licked her hand. She laughed as he turned and ran behind his mother, only to peer out from beneath his mother's belly, then he wandered back up to Jesse and did the whole thing over again.

Jesse was so caught up in playing with the foal that she didn't realize Justin was standing at the door watching her until he spoke.

"He's cute isn't he?" Justin asked. When he brought the fresh water back, he hadn't expected Jessica to be up, let alone crouched down in the stall with Maggie and her baby. She didn't strike him as the type of woman who would crouch down in the stall of a mare and play with her foal. She seemed more like the self-absorbed snobby sort just like Annie had been.

When he saw her gelding and stud had been fed he knew she was up and about. He had wanted to turn around right there and head home but he had to finish chores. He didn't want anything to do with her, or any other woman for that matter.

Startled, Jesse stood abruptly, sending the foal back to his mother for protection. "You scared me. Yes, he is cute. Is he out of the stallion just down the aisle, To Catch a Reason, I believe was his name?" she asked.

"Yes he is. We call the stallion Catchy." Justin opened the door and put the bucket of water inside. "Don't forget to lock the door when you leave," he barked as he turned and strode from the barn.

"Wow, what nerve!" Jesse thought as she opened the door and stepped from the stall. One quick glance back at the foal and then she walked toward the house. Justin acted like he owned the place, giving orders to close and lock the door, like she was an idiot or something.

She saw a light on in the kitchen and realized Mary was probably cooking breakfast. Jesse used to sit and watch Mary cook for all the ranch hands when she was a kid and sometimes she was even allowed to help Mary cook. In a strange way, having Mary just inside cooking breakfast made it seem to Jesse like she was finally home to a real family even though it wasn't her mom and dad.

After giving her boots a quick check for manure she entered and smiled as Mary bustled around the kitchen. The whole house smelled of frying bacon and coffee. Mary's thin frame turned and faced Jesse. As she did, her thin face widened.

"Jessica Walker, you are a welcome surprise. We're so glad to have you back."

Mary was a rather tough woman who you usually didn't want to mess with. She was never mean, just very proper and tough. When Jesse was a kid, her mother used to tell her how Mary had won a shooting competition against ten men and that she had rode bulls when she was younger. Jesse couldn't believe it was the same woman who stood in her kitchen before her cooking breakfast. Mary wrapped her arms around Jesse and to Jesse's surprise she still felt as strong as she always had been.

Stepping back and returning to her task of getting breakfast ready Mary asked about all that was happening in Jesse's life. Jesse and Mary talked about Hank and Logan and occasionally Justin's name came up. Mary told Jesse that Justin needed to find a wife and settle down. Jesse laughed as she realized nothing had changed around the Running W no matter what else had changed in the world. Mary was still trying to find everyone a mate—to be married was to be happy was her motto. If only she had met Hank in the past few years she would know that to be married wasn't quite good enough.

Jesse told Mary about her phone call from Jack. Mary's face went grim, but she just turned around and poured a cup of coffee. After handing it to Jesse she replied. "Jack has been different lately. He seems like maybe he is a little depressed or something. So do me a favor and be nice to him." Mary poured herself a cup of hot black coffee and sat at the table across from Jesse, waiting for the bacon to finish frying.

"I will be nice to him, Mary. I sure as heck didn't come back to start a fight with anyone. If we have a good lunch, maybe I will invite him out to supper sometime," Jesse stated, even to her surprise.

"Oh, that would be nice. I don't think he gets out much anymore." Mary stood and began to pull the bacon from the frying pan. "Would you call Logan and Justin in for breakfast, please, Jessica?"

Jesse opened the door and rang the big chimes on the porch. The chimes sent memories flooding back from her childhood. Her mom used to use these chimes because she couldn't yell very loud. Her father had bought them for her mother for Christmas one year. Her mother had been outraged after opening her gift up and finding a large set of dinner chimes, until he had laughed and brought a small box out from under the tree, wrapped in shiny paper and tied with a bow. It contained a beautiful locket, which she had always cherished.

"Come and get it," she yelled just for the fun of it.

The chimes sent birds flying and made the horses quit eating and look up. It didn't last long before their heads dropped again and they went back to eating on the new spring growth. Jesse loved this time of year when everything was green and smelled new. The trees bloomed, the grass grew, birds chirped high above and the bees hummed as they pollinated the flowers that had just bloomed beside the steps.

Her thoughts were interrupted when she saw Justin and Logan emerge from the new barn and walk toward the house. She couldn't help but stare at the way Justin walked across the driveway. His demeanor was that of an old western cowboy. His white T-shirt showed a little dirt from something he had to move that morning with his shoulder, his faded Wranglers were showing their many washings. One wash had finally caught up with them and caused a small fray by his knee, which caught Jesse's attention as she watched his long legs move. She turned and went back inside to help Mary set the table; she didn't want anyone to see her gawking at Justin.

Breakfast was quiet on Jesse's part, as she was too busy downing one of the best meals she had had in a long time. Her thoughts were on what Jack might be like now. She also wanted to go drive around and look at a few of her old memories before she had to go to lunch.

Between mouthfuls she said, "Hey Logan, before I go to lunch, I think I'm going to go look around the area this morning."

"Lunch? Who you going to lunch with?" Logan asked.

"Jack called and asked me to lunch," Jesse replied.

"Jack who?" Logan asked.

"Jack Smith."

"Oh well, I hope you two have fun at lunch. Where you two heading?"

"Grandma's Café," Jesse replied.

"Good. You know Betty still owns that. She outlasted many of the town folk at their businesses. I'm proud of her. She even refused to sell to the newcomers, who I heard offered her a very pretty penny."

Logan knew Jack and Jessica used to be somewhat of an item before Hank. He was glad to see her getting out but he wasn't sure Jack was the best type of guy anymore. But he figured Jack wouldn't hurt Jesse and she was just having lunch with him.

"What are you planning today, Justin?" Logan asked.

"I'm going to finish up the rest of that fence. I found a few more downed trees I want to cut away." Justin didn't like Jack at all. He and Jack had had a run-in a few years ago at the bar. Ever since, Justin hadn't cared to ever see him again. The idea of Jessica eating lunch with the guy didn't settle well with him at all. He would rather she have lunch with a rattlesnake than Jack Smith; he knew they were one and the same. He stood up from his half-empty plate.

"If you don't mind, I'm not very hungry this morning. I'll just wrap it up and eat it for lunch."

Mary looked at him but didn't say a word. She just stood up and got a plastic container from the cupboard for Justin's food. After emptying his plate and adding a few more pieces of bacon, some chips, a candy bar, and a drink, she placed it in a bag and wished him a good day.

"Be careful up there, Justin, and don't forget to stop and eat that lunch." Justin sighed; twice he had forgotten to stop for lunch in all the past nine and a half years and his grandmother hadn't let him forget it.

"Yes, Grandma, I will. See you for dinner," he said as he kissed Mary on the cheek and headed for the door.

Justin cursed as he descended the steps and made his way across the driveway to his truck. "Jack had better stay far away from me. I have no use for the bastard or his antics." He jumped in his truck and roared up the mountain. Good hard work would relieve most of his frustrations.

If he were a drinking man, a shot of whiskey would probably have helped. Unfortunately, he wasn't into drinking. In fact he had no bad habits he could think of; he didn't smoke or drink, he didn't beat or abuse women. He was a nice guy all in all, but he couldn't figure out why he was blessed with such bad luck. First Annie, then his parents, and now a woman boss who had to be beautiful.

He just hoped that she didn't end up with Jack as a permanent boyfriend. There was no way on earth he was going to take orders from Jack Smith. A woman was bad, but he was ten times worse.

Jesse helped clean up after breakfast and then jumped in her own truck and headed for the highway. She drove around all morning looking over the old homesteads and remembering everything that made Danville home to her.

The old tree swing that hung out over the river was gone; the tree had been cut down. The bridge they used to party under was so rickety now she didn't even dare to cross it in her truck. The school looked the same, but the children who were playing out in the playground didn't look anything like her when she was little. The little girls were wearing tight pants and short shirts. The boys had long hair or greasy spikes. The older children had tattoos and earrings placed in rather odd places on their faces.

She thought to herself, "Wow, times have sure changed. When I was a kid only bulls had nose rings."

Driving through town again she stopped in front of the old saddle shop and wondered if Bill still owned it. She pulled up to the curb, stepped out, and watched the people carefully as they bustled around the streets. These people moved so fast. They never slowed down to look at whom they passed or to say hello to anyone.

She didn't trust a one of them, and wasn't going to relax around them either. If what Logan had said was true there wasn't one of them she could trust and she didn't plan on trying to get to know any of them. She opened the door and walked into the saddle shop. The place smelled of wet leather. She heard some voices coming from the back room. It sounded like someone was arguing back behind the curtain; Jesse knew that was Bill's workshop back there.

"Bill!" Jesse yelled. An older man with graying hair came into view. Jesse recognized Bill instantly. A younger man with a dark beard and a long ponytail came from the back room as well. He looked at Jesse and hurried out the door.

"May I help you, young lady?" Bill asked.

"It's me, Bill, Jesse Walker." Jesse couldn't believe Bill had forgotten her. She had spent a lot of her days right back there behind those curtains watching Bill build saddles.

"Yes, Jesse. What can I do for you?" Bill replied. His old eyes gave a little twinkle; he smiled and repeated the same sentence.

"I just wanted to say hi."

"Oh good. Goodbye then, young lady, I have work to do."

Jesse knew something wasn't right. So she figured she would say it a little quieter just in case.

"Bill, is everything okay?" Jesse whispered.

Bill nodded and tossed his head toward the curtains, and Jesse knew he remembered her but didn't want to say so out loud. Jesse realized there was someone else back in the back room who Bill didn't want to know they knew each other.

"What can I do for you, young lady?" Bill smiled as he said it this time.

"I want you to build a saddle for me," Jesse lied. "I need a new barrel saddle, size fourteen seat. Can you manage?"

"Yes, you'll have to come back later for fittings and to tell me about details. I have company right now and I'll need a couple hours of your time for details," Bill stated.

Jesse agreed and left the saddle shop. She didn't like the way Bill was acting, but she would talk more to him later. Right now she figured she had better get to Grandma's Café before she was late for lunch.

She strode down the street and opened the door to the old weather-sided café. Everything looked the same: the old barstools lined the counter in front of her, their leather seats cracked and worn from years of use. The booths lined the two walls to her left and right. The center was strewn with smaller tables for one or two people. She waited for her eyes to get totally adjusted to the dim light of the café before she looked around for Jack.

She knew she was about ten minutes early and after no luck in finding anyone who resembled him she chose a booth and sat facing the door. Within seconds a slender woman who

Jesse guessed had to be in her mid-forties came, gave her a menu, and placed a glass of ice water in front of her.

"Can I get you something to drink?" the lady asked.

"Pepsi please," Jesse said as she turned back to the door. Out in the street she could see people walking. She looked for anyone that resembled what Jack might look like.

A big black Ford pickup pulled up and parked in her view. Dang it, she thought, now I can't see anything. The door opened and out stepped a tall, broad-chested man who had definitely worked out a few days in his life. The man wore black jeans and a stark white T-shirt.

He turned and Jesse gasped, "Jack." He wasn't at all the same man she remembered. He was eighteen the last time she saw him, skinny build and unruly blond hair.

He pushed open the door and swept into the room like a fresh breeze. Jesse couldn't believe the change in him. His face looked like a statue, his eyes were still the same steel blue, but his jaw was much squarer than she remembered. His face looked hard and smooth. He wore no expression as he glanced around the room. He smiled as his eyes came to rest on her.

Jack had always loved Jesse and had resented her for choosing Hank over him. Now he had another chance to make her see that she still needed him. He strolled over and took a seat across the table from her.

She looked good. Tired, but good.

"Jack, you look so different. I hardly recognized you," Jesse exclaimed.

"Jesse, you look the same as I remember you, beautiful in every way." Jack's eyes softened as he said words he hoped would flatter her and win her back into his arms.

They spent most of the afternoon talking and laughing. Jesse was starting to wonder why she had ever thought Jack was too much like a brother figure. He was so fun to be around. She loved the way his eyes danced when he spoke of their past.

They were so caught up in talking that she hadn't realized the rest of the café had cleared out. The skinny waitress stood at their table informing them they had to leave because the café was closing.

"Already? They used to keep this place open till six," Jesse exclaimed.

The waitress smiled warmly. "It's six thirty. I let you two talk until I got through cleaning up. You've been here for seven hours."

Jesse gasped in disbelief. "I'm so sorry to inconvenience you," Jesse apologized as she stood next to Jack as he covered the bill and tipped the waitress twenty dollars. They turned and left the café. Once outside she turned to Jack.

"I guess I had better get home. Would you like to come for dinner some night?" Jesse asked.

"I would love to," Jack answered as he stepped closer. He lowered his head and brushed his lips to hers. As soon as it had started, it ended. The brief kiss had nothing in it. Jesse smiled as she turned and walked to her truck.

After reading all those romance books of Marnie's she had half expected the kiss to send tingles up and down her spine. At least she hoped it would. Somehow she felt almost disappointed she hadn't felt anything in that brief kiss.

She hadn't got to talk to Bill but she promised herself she would stop by in the next couple days and see what the talk of the town was. He had always been a good friend of her father and would tell her what was going on in her hometown. Maybe he would have an idea of who was behind all the problems it now faced.

She knew she was going to have to address the situation at some point, she just hoped she could get settled in before she had to make too many people hate her.

She hoped she could count on Jack and Logan and maybe even Justin to back her up if trouble started. Marnie was always so sweet and kind, and Jesse worried about her coming on Friday. Jesse hoped she could keep her out of whatever trouble there was in the town. In fact she hoped she could stay out of all the trouble in the town, too.

She couldn't figure out how something like this happened in her old hometown without someone shooting everyone involved. When she was a kid everyone had a gun handy in their truck and everyone, even children, knew how to use one.

She remembered a peddler that had come to town trying to sell his wares one day. He camped down by the river on state land, set up his stand, and started to sell his trinkets. Within minutes of hearing of this her father, mother, and every neighbor she knew drove down there to tell him to move along. His kind wasn't needed there, and they saw him to the county line.

Her drive back to the ranch was unsettling as she thought of this cult thing. Jesse tried desperately to think of why the town folk let it get to be so big of a problem that disappearances and killings were taking place.

She worried about Bill. What if the person in the back was one of the killers?

Chapter 4

Back at the ranch she fed Cozy and Boe a treat and ate a quick sandwich with Logan. He told her about a couple new calves and a new foal. She took note to make sure she would take a look at the foal in the morning; tonight she just wanted to go have some fun and go riding for a while.

Jesse put her dishes in the sink and placed Logan's on top. She would get back to them when she got home later. Turning to where Logan sat at the table letting his food settle she said, "I'm going to go saddle up Cozy and take him for a ride. I feel like stretching my legs a little and I'm sure he would like to as well." Jesse missed just getting on and riding for no good reason at all. With Hank it was always, "If you want to be the best, you will practice more, Jess. Practice, practice, practice." And that was all she had done.

"Sounds like a good idea. Have fun, and remember what I said, stick to Running W land." Logan stood and walked from the kitchen without another word. Jesse grabbed her baseball cap and, pulling her braid through the hole in back, placed it on her head.

Once she had Cozy saddled and led from the breezeway she mounted and turned him up the road past the barn and toward the north range. She knew Justin might be up there, but with any luck she wouldn't run in to him or anyone else. She just wanted to be alone tonight and ride. Logan had done a good job of scaring her. She knew she would probably not want to talk to anyone around here ever again.

While she rode, her thoughts went from one thing to another. Hank and all his ways were always tormenting her something fierce. But most of all she worried about Marnie driving up by herself, but she had to put that thought in the back of her head. She wanted to enjoy her ride, and worrying wasn't going to help her do that at all.

She thought about Jack and that brief kiss. He had been so fun and carefree, not at all like when they were dating. He used to be so strained to talk to. His thoughts would come and go and were mostly centered on sports or sex when they were kids. Maybe he was just trying to impress her, maybe he hadn't changed all that much after all. Oh well, she would have plenty of time to find out this summer. She didn't think she would mind getting to know him a little better.

Once through the upper gate, she gave Cozy the reins, and leaned forward over his neck and let him run free. He stood on his back legs and lunged forward into a fast gallop across the meadow. Jesse dropped even lower on his neck and felt him kick up his hind feet. It had been a long time since they both just ran with no direction in life. It felt great to be free.

She felt the wind hit her face, and all her cares melted away. She stretched out along his neck and Cozy went faster than Jesse could ever remember. The trees were a blur, the wind made her eyes water, but she promised Cozy he could run all he wanted. He slowed a little and gave a nicker, and Jesse laughed—she guessed he wanted to kick up his heels and yell at the wind as well.

As they neared the tree line, Jesse pulled Cozy up to a walk. He pranced and tossed his head at the change in pace.

"Easy, boy, save some energy. I don't want you to knock me off with a tree branch," Jesse explained as she steered him through the trees. The forest was so quiet not a bird sang, or anything else.

Suddenly alarmed at that fact, she pulled Cozy to a halt, and listened for any sign of life. She wished she had thought to grab a gun from her dad's gun cabinet. She wasn't the greatest shot, but she could usually hit what she aimed at.

She knew Justin might be up here somewhere, but he would be along one of the fences, not out in the middle of the forest. Jesse knew mountain lions roamed here as well, but Cozy wasn't acting like anything dangerous was about. She figured it must be a human. Cozy's ears shot up; he heard something straight ahead.

Then she heard it too. What was it? Clop, clop, clop. It sounded like hoof beats or pounding of some kind. She knew Logan had said not to talk to strangers but surely she could spy on them from a distance. She eased Cozy toward the noise.

Whatever it was it had suddenly stopped, so she inched closer. Her breath caught in her throat. She stepped off Cozy and hunched down, crawling closer still, and watched.

Justin stopped chopping long enough to wipe the sweat from his brow, and looked back up the fence line toward the truck. It was just about a mile out of sight and he wished it wasn't quite so far from this damn downed tree. The fence was down flat and he had left the chainsaw back at the ranch.

He was in so much of a hurry to get out of there he might have forgotten his head had it not been attached. Damn Jessica for talking about Jack and damn him for letting it get to him so much. She was a big girl and she could do what she wanted.

With all the killings and strange happenings one didn't want to stray too far from the escape that his pickup offered. He was good at fighting and he was a crack shot with the .30-06 that lay across a stump to his right, but still he didn't have a great feeling about being up there so close to dark.

It usually got dark around nine thirty. It was now about a quarter to seven or so. So he knew he had a little more time to finish up with the tree and get back before dark. Two years ago his hired hand Andrew had been shot and killed just down the fence line about two hundred yards. They found his horse the next morning.

The buzzards had eaten out its eyes and a lot of his neck but not a drop of blood stained the ground. The poor horse had been drained of all his blood and sexual organs. Search parties looked everywhere for Andrew, with no luck until last year when a hunter came across some remains up on Forest Service land. They were confirmed to be his.

The sheriff said it may have been a cougar, but everyone knew what had happened. It was murder. In fact, it had been happening a lot in the past few years. He didn't like the fact that Jessica had come into the mix; she could get hurt or killed. That thought didn't settle well with him. He didn't know her but he sure as hell didn't want her dying. He turned his thoughts back to the task at hand.

He had noticed this old tree leaning toward the fence last fall while chasing cows up here, but forgot to come back up and fall it away. Sometime last winter the snow or wind had made the tree fall, and right down on the fence, of course. So now he had the task of chopping it off the fence before the cows could be turned out, and fixing the fence back up afterward.

He was having problems getting Jessica out of his thoughts. She was pretty, he had to give her that. She seemed nice enough, but so had Annie in the beginning. Annie was the sweetest person alive, so everyone had told him. They still tell him to this day when he sees his old friends who knew them as a couple.

Logan always asks, "What happened to that sweet little girl you were engaged to?" Justin's friends from back home seem to call every week and just happen to have seen her out on the town or at a grocery store and wonder why Justin ever let her get away.

She had fooled him, too. On the outside, she was so sweet, kind, and caring. Love was her only goal in life, she used to say. That was until Justin's parents' untimely death left Justin with a million dollar inheritance.

Justin had never known his parents; they were too busy for him so they had sent him to be raised by his father's sister, Iris. Justin saw his parents maybe once a year, and after his tenth birthday he never cared to see them again.

The only thing they did for him was to help him see what kind of a person Annie really was before he married her. He thanked them for that. That sweet little woman turned into a money-hungry hog. If his friends could afford her, they could have her with his blessings.

"Oh yeah, she's sweet all right. Like a baby rattler with his first button, she's sweet. The bitch. That's what she is and what most women turn into with time." Justin wanted to kick himself for believing that he had found the woman of his dreams in Annie.

He knew he never wanted to be loved or love another woman for as long as he lived. Annie had taught him a good lesson. He wouldn't mind a woman of the night now and then just for a pleasurable roll, but he never wanted to see her again after he rolled over.

He wished Jessica was one of those women, with her long, sleek body that he could enjoy all night long. Her long dark hair loose and falling over her shoulders. His name on her lips. Just thinking of her made his blood heat up and his loins react.

Good God, Justin. Has it been that long since you had a woman that only the thought of a woman makes you hard? he asked himself.

Get your mind off Jessica. She isn't for you, he told himself. He worked harder and the sweat poured down his bare chest. He had long since shed his shirt to keep cool in the heat of the setting sun.

She wasn't for Jack, either, and he wished he could stop her from doing something stupid. She was probably wrapped up in his arms right now. That vision hit him harder than he thought it would. He felt betrayed by a woman he didn't even know. How could that happen? A part of him wanted to go find Jack and kick his ass yet again.

A sudden movement to his right caught Justin's attention. He was over the log with his rifle and fired a warning shot before he realized what was happening. He couldn't believe he had let his guard down. He could have been killed before he ever knew what was happening.

"The next shot will hit you right between the eyes if you don't show yourself," Justin yelled as he cocked another bullet into the chamber of his rifle and leveled it at the bushes.

"Justin, don't shoot! It's me, Jesse!" Jesse was a little scared as she led Cozy from the bushes. She had been watching him work for some time and hadn't realized he had seen her until he shot above her. Her feet trembled and she was finding it hard to breathe when she reached him at the tree.

She had been so intent on watching him work. He was stunning, every muscle tensed across his chest and down his back as he swung the ax. The setting sun made his flesh shimmer. He was magnificent and she was lost in the movement of his body.

"You could have been killed sneaking around in the bushes. What are you doing out here alone?" Justin lectured. He watched in amusement as her lower lip trembled. He had scared her pretty bad he guessed.

"Are you going to answer me?" he asked. He was bound and determined not to back down. She could have been killed. What would she have done if it weren't him out here?

"I was riding." Jesse was trying hard to get ahold of her emotions.

Justin didn't soften one bit. "Hasn't Logan told you about all that's been going on around here?"

"Yes, and will you please stop yelling at me? I'm sorry. I didn't know who you were, that's why I was sneaking up on you," Jesse stammered.

Justin was starting to see a scared little child in front of him. The tough hard businesswoman was a front to the scared little child that stood before him now. A slight smile touched his lip, but he quickly wiped it away.

Jesse saw it before it vanished; the slightest uplift to the corners of his mouth made his hardened features look boyish in the setting sun. She wanted to say something to make it return, but could think of nothing to say except, "Is there anything I can do to help?"

"Do you know how to run a pair of fence stretchers?" he asked. Justin figured he had better put her to work before she started crying and he had to console her. Crying women were his only weakness. He had always hated to see a woman cry.

"It's been a while but I think I can manage." Jesse grabbed the fence stretchers and started hooking them up to the fence. A couple cranks were all she could manage with the brush in her face. The fence was by no means tight, so she tried to crank some more. She pushed the brush out of her way but it snapped back and stung her face.

"Damn brush!" Jesse cursed under her breath as she rubbed her cheek against the stinging pain.

"Here, let me help you a little." Jesse stepped aside as Justin grabbed a handful of brush and pulled it out by its roots. "There, now try it." Justin looked at her face—it was turning red where the brush had hit it.

"Let me look at your cheek." He turned her face with his gloved hand and examined the marks. His fingers moved up her cheek. Jesse looked into his face. His eyes were so blue, a light blue, almost as if there was no color at all. They were fantastic and captivating. His face was tanned and looked a lot tougher than Jack's, yet there was a tenderness in his face she had never seen in anyone else's as far back as she could remember, except maybe her own father's.

"Just stings, no blood, you'll be fine. It might be red for a couple hours," Justin explained. As he stepped back he was glad for the layer of leather his gloves provided between his hands and her skin. It looked so soft and touchable.

"Thanks. Justin, could I ask you a few questions while we work? It might make the time go by quicker if you don't mind," Jesse said. She wanted to know so much about what had been happening around here, and about him. He struck her curiosity right square on the bull's-eye.

"I guess. What do you want to know?" Justin wondered what he could possibly know that would interest Jessica.

"Is Logan your real grandpa?" Justin looked at her quizzically. That was not the question he thought she would ask at all.

"Yes he is. Why?" Justin stopped moving chunks of tree out of the trail and looked at her strangely.

"Curiosity, that's all. You don't act like him." Jesse had to test him out and see what kind of a guy Justin was, and this was the perfect time. He couldn't run away.

"Well, he is my real grandpa. What is it to you?" Justin was already tired of this conversation and he hoped his tone would change that.

"I was just curious, don't yell at me. You're very trying. Do you know that?" Jesse didn't give him time to answer. "It's just that Logan is so friendly and talkative and you're like getting to know a water moccasin." Jesse laughed to herself. Justin didn't like to talk about himself at all and she found that funny.

Jesse tested the fence strength and said, "Done."

She stepped back and admired her fencing job. Not as pretty as she had seen Logan do, but not bad. Out of the corner of her eye, she saw Justin looking at her and smiling.

"What?" Jesse said.

"Nothing at all. I have a question for you, Jessica," Justin said as he cleared the last of the brush away from the trail.

"Call me Jesse, please. What is it you want to know?"

"Why are you here? Why did you come back to Danville?" Justin asked. The sudden look of sadness in her face made him wish he hadn't asked the question. Justin sat on the end of the tree and took a swig of water. "I'm sorry, it's none of my business. If it's painful you don't have to talk about it." Justin added, "I'm one person who knows how it feels to be pushed into answering questions. I don't want to push anyone else into answering something they don't want to."

Jesse watched as a small trickle of water dripped down his chin and ran down his bare chest. She watched as it made its way toward his waist only to soak into his jeans. Suddenly, as she realized the direction she was looking, she jerked her head up and saw his eyes watching her in playful humor.

"It's not painful really. I guess, my husband thinks marriage is a three-person thing, and I don't. I had nowhere else to go but home," Jesse explained without the details, and then added another question. "Are you married?"

"Married? No way, not me!" Justin exclaimed.

"Smart man," Jesse acknowledged. "Well, shouldn't we be getting home before somebody who actually doesn't like us shoots at us?"

Justin smiled. Maybe she really wasn't so bad. She could be a fun person to work with this summer and she was sure a lot prettier to look at than Logan.

"Yes. I guess we'd better go. Do you want to tie your gelding to the truck and ride with me down to the ranch?"

"Tempting, but if you don't mind I would rather ride Cozy. I think he's smoother to sit on than that old truck." Jesse had seen his truck, a late eighties Ford pickup with about as much shock absorption left as she had testosterone.

"Suit yourself, Jesse, but would you mind staying with the truck so I don't have to worry about you getting back all right?" Justin asked.

"I guess I could do that." Jesse mounted Cozy and followed as Justin gathered the fencing supplies and started walking to the truck.

"Cozy rides double if you would like to ride up the hill instead of walk."

"Sounds good to me," Justin said. He handed the fencing equipment to Jesse and slung his rifle over his shoulder. With a quick leap, he was behind Jesse and she could feel his hard body just inches away.

They didn't talk much as they made their way up the hill. Jesse knew her voice would give away her thoughts, and right now those were not good religious thoughts.

He smelled good, the scent of pine and sweat. He smelled all man and in her state of thinking that might be dangerous to her safe being. She would have to make sure to keep her distance from Justin in the future.

Back at the truck, Justin stepped down and relieved Jesse of the fencing equipment. "Thanks for the ride, I'll see you at the ranch."

With that, Justin turned and placed the equipment in the bed of the truck and got in. His heart was racing as he watched her ride down the road ahead of him, her hips swaying with the rhythm of her gelding's movements.

If he wasn't careful he was going to have to start bringing ice water with him to dump over himself. He started the engine and followed at a safe distance behind her as she made her way back to the ranch.

* * *

A lone rider sat watching from on top of the cliff. The big bay snorted as the big man replaced the rifle into the scabbard and mounted.

"Another day I will make you sorry."

He turned the bay and sunk the silver spurs into the bay's already raw sides. The bay shot into the tree line and toward home.

Chapter 5

Back at the ranch Jesse spent a little extra time brushing Cozy. For fifteen years he was a great horse, and she loved him more than anything else in the world. He turned his head from his oats and nickered as Logan stepped into the stall.

"Supper is ready when you get done. Mary went ahead and cooked over at your place again, steak and potatoes with corn on the cob, I think." He looked at Jesse and Cozy and thought of the day her dad had given her that colt.

The little girl, who now stood before him all grown up, had stepped from the house to find, tied to the front porch rail, a little colt with a big red bow around his neck. The smile on her face was the biggest he had ever seen in his life. Logan had watched her break him and make him the horse he was today and he watched as that little colt made her the woman she had become today.

"He's been a good horse for you, hasn't he?"

"You remember him. I thought maybe you forgot about him." Jesse was shocked to find out that Logan remembered Cozy.

"I've been following you and that horse's progress ever since you left this ranch," Logan stated and turned to go. "You dropped his shoulder in Denver three years ago, he didn't do it on his own. You were lucky you won that one. And lucky he's such a good horse and picked it up on his own." Logan walked out of the stall and started down the breezeway.

"How do you know that? That event wasn't televised," Jesse yelled down the aisle after his disappearing silhouette.

She remembered that event well. She had a huge fight with Hank. He had accidentally hit her and blackened her right eye right behind the bucking chutes and she was having a horrible time of seeing anything out of it.

Running barrels had been almost impossible. She hadn't been able to judge distance or rate. Cozy had done it all on his own that day and they still won.

Without even slowing, Logan spouted, "Row three, seat twelve. I should have killed the bastard that day and saved you a heartache later."

Jesse's heart sank. He had been there, and he saw the whole thing. She closed Cozy's stall and headed for the house. Hank had only hit her twice in their whole life together, that time and one other when she had spilled his food accidentally. He apologized and begged for forgiveness both times, and Jesse was so dumb and naive that she believed him yet again. Jesse ended up telling everybody she had fallen, and forgave Hank yet again.

The evening meal went without a hitch. The conversation was light-hearted and fun as Logan teased Mary about her cooking. Justin and Jesse joined in and laughed as Mary dumped a glass of water over Logan's head.

After dinner, Jesse helped Mary clean up and wash dishes. They all said their goodnights and ambled in their own directions. Logan and Mary to the bunkhouse, Justin toward the Lawson place, and Jesse to her bedroom.

She tossed and turned well into the night before she finally gave up and turned on a light and pulled out a book, *To Love With Half A Heart*. She had been reading this book for some time now and wasn't quite sure how she got started on it. It was definitely an unusual story that had little to do with anything in her own life, unlike the ones she usually read about—a rodeo cowboy or a girl who ran the circuit and loved a man she couldn't have.

Instead, she read about some poor man who lost his heart to a devil of a woman and now refused to love again with all his heart. Oh, he had lots of women, slept with a different woman almost every night. Tonight she read about Amber the cocktail waitress who seduced him with her short skirt and low top, ample bosom (whatever that meant) and nightly ways.

She found herself wishing she had a glossary of terms found in romance books so she could fully understand what was happening. She wondered if Marnie had kept the glossary that came with this book. Marnie was always giving her these kinds of books. Jesse teased Marnie about the books being the reason she wasn't married yet. She was setting her standards too high; no man was ever as sweet and romantic as they were in her books. Love was more complicated in real life than the books made it out to be, and once they slept together everything was great after that. No more fights, no more crying in the middle of the night when he didn't come home from a rodeo he was due home from hours before. Knowing deep down he was out with some nightly harlot who was teaching him a thing or two in her own way.

Marnie had made a joke out of Jesse actually finishing one of those books. For each book Jesse read, Marnie would give her a little cow figurine and write the name of the book on the underside. Jesse loved the little cows, so she kept reading the books, and she enjoyed the books, too. In some strange way she would never admit to anyone, it was nice to think of a place where love actually could be like it was in the stories, if only for a moment.

The men were always so sweet, romantic, and always there in time to save the girl in trouble. The women were always young, firm, gorgeous, and would always go numb and forget the world around them when the big, strong, handsome man rode up on his big, strong steed and kissed her beyond reason. The world would spin around and fireworks would light up the sky.

Sex was called "lovemaking" and it always took more than five minutes. Afterwards the couple would snuggle and fall asleep in each other's arms as opposed to the man rolling over and looking for the remote that had been poking the woman in the back the whole time.

Hank never kissed her and never said any romantic things, except maybe "Get me some food," or "Did you feed the damn dog?" If that was romance then she had been romanced for the last ten years. However, romance was a fairy tale to her. No dashing men ever rode up and saved her when Hank hit her behind the chutes. She never felt the earth tremble or forgot what she was doing with Hank.

Lovemaking with Hank had been like supper—it didn't matter what you wanted. If he wanted it, he got it. He would get what he wanted and then roll over and go to sleep. There was never any romantic talk or snuggling, not even in the beginning.

She read about all the shivering and shaking, which to her had only happened if Hank wanted sex outside in the barn and it was cold. He would get on, do his thing, and get off. If she were lucky, she would only miss about five minutes of her television show.

She found herself wondering what Justin would be like in bed. She remembered how he felt behind her on Cozy; he was so hard and strong. Yet he was kind, too. She could tell when he touched her cheek with his gloved hand that he truly cared if she was okay. It was a new feeling for Jesse to know that someone actually cared if she was hurt.

She wondered if he was dating anyone from around here. She knew he wasn't married, but with a body and heart like his he couldn't be single very long. When she walked into the house for supper she had heard Mary tell Justin some woman by the name of Karla had called and wanted him to go dancing with her.

She felt a tinge of jealousy. The thought of him in another woman's arms made her green with envy. She almost wanted to pick up the phone and call him to see if he was home alone, but she knew it was none of her business.

"Stop it, Jess, you can't expect him to want you," she told herself. "A man like him, I'm sure he has somebody."

Jesse read a few more pages and drifted off to sleep. She missed morning and slept well into the two o'clock hour. She might have slept longer had Justin not knocked on her bedroom door.

"Hey, you alive in there? It's two in the afternoon. You have a couple of cows that disappeared. You want to help me look for them?" Justin hadn't wanted to ask Jesse to come along, but Logan insisted that he do so. It was two in the afternoon and she still slept. Last night, from his bed, he had been able to see her bedroom window. He watched the light come on after midnight and was aware of it being on until two-thirty or so, when sleep claimed him again.

He found it hard to sleep with her light on. He wondered if she stayed awake worrying about her soon to be ex-husband or if she lay awake fantasizing about Jack. He hoped she had seen Jack for what he was worth, and told him to go straight to hell.

He didn't need the distraction and really didn't want her along with him today. The last thing he needed was her looking so damn good that he wanted to change his future plans. She was a nice person, but still, she had a lot of needs and she was going to need a lot more if she didn't get out of bed soon or at least answer him.

"Hey, are you getting up or am I going to have to break down this door and drag you out?" He hated waiting for women to get ready. Even if all she was going to do was lay around the house, Annie took about two hours every morning to put on her makeup and get dressed.

The door swung open and Jesse stepped out, dressed in faded Wranglers a white T-shirt and her baseball hat.

"Good morning to you, too," Jesse teased. "Aren't you up bright and early."

"You sleep all day at home, too?" Justin asked bitterly. Justin was shocked to see her already dressed, no makeup, and ready to go. But she did smell good, of apples and vanilla.

"This is home. And no, not usually, but I didn't sleep very well last night." She wouldn't mention the reason was him. "The mattress was lumpy," she lied.

"Oh well, I guess we'd better take care of that." He smirked as thoughts of him helping her flatten it out ran across his mind. He suddenly changed his mind's direction when he saw her watching him with curious eyes the color of a river stream.

"Some of the cows disappeared last night. I found a hole in the fence up on the east side and thought you might want to go riding."

"I'd love to. I'll go get my horse saddled."

"I already saddled your gelding, and mine, too, so if you're ready, let's go." Justin turned and started downstairs without looking back.

"What? I don't even get it brought to the front door?" Jesse teased.

"No, nor do I do laundry or wash dishes."

"You smell pretty good for a man who never washes his laundry." Jesse smiled as she saw him do a double take.

"Funny. Are you always so funny?"

"You know what they say, looks aren't everything."

"I have never heard a woman say that before."

"You hang with the wrong type of women, then."

"Maybe."

Jesse followed him down the stairs and out the front door. She stepped up beside him as they strode across the driveway to where Cozy and a big gray gelding stood waiting. Justin had a long stride, she would grant him that. She found it hard to keep up with him.

Jesse tightened her cinch and, stepping up on Cozy, she watched as Justin mounted the gray. She could tell the gray had a lot of power; his chest was broad and deep. This was as nice of a put together horse as she had ever seen.

She had remembered the gray in the stall; his nameplate read "Badger." She also remembered him not being very sociable, and now she saw why. He was Justin's horse, and a reflection of his owner.

"That's a nice gelding. Where did you get him?" Jesse asked, trying to kill the silence. "Not too many horses around these parts look like him." She knew he must be well bred and highly valuable.

"I raised him from a baby. He's out of my stallion and a Flying M mare I bought from Monroe's farm." Jesse knew the Monroes; they had good stock. Expensive, but good. Cozy matched the gray stride for stride.

They turned and rode side by side up the road past the barn and toward the north range. If a cow had gotten out on the east side, that meant she was up in the Forest Service area. Through the north range was the only way up.

"Justin, should we have brought a lunch?" Jesse asked.

Justin laughed. "No, but maybe dinner. Remember it's around two o'clock, sleepyhead?"

They rode in silence through the north range, looking back and forth, stopping often to listen for any noise that might mean they needed to be alarmed. Jesse knew Justin was on edge and tried to make herself invisible by staying directly behind him.

Justin led them around the clearing and through the trees. He sat tall and erect on the gray's back. The gray seemed to never miss a beat. Over logs and around rocks, higher and higher they rode. Jesse knew the Forest Service gate was just around the bend.

Justin stopped and stepped off the gray, threw a stirrup up over the saddle horn, and tightened his cinch. Then, after lowering his stirrup, he turned, walked back to Jesse, and checked her cinch.

"Move your leg back and I'll tighten yours as well," he whispered, barely loud enough for Jesse to hear. Jesse felt his hand against her calf as he pushed her leg aside and jerked the cinch tight. She looked down onto the brim of his cowboy hat and then to his broad shoulders.

He was strong and silent, just the way a cowboy should be. She held her leg back out of the way. He was too much of a temptation for her to be touching. She had never felt that way about any man, even Hank. But Justin, she wanted to touch him more than anything just to know what his skin felt like against her own flesh. She knew it would feel warm from all the sun it had soaked up. But was it as soft and smooth as it looked?

Justin finished tightening her cinch and looked up to find her staring down at him. Her face showed mixed emotions. One he could read very well, curiosity. The same emotion he was dealing with right now. He wondered what she would do if he pulled her out of her saddle and kissed her long and hard.

By the look on her face he knew what she would do, but he knew it couldn't happen or he would never forgive himself. She wasn't a one-night stand type of woman, and he wasn't a forever type of guy. He could look at her and dream of her but he knew he could never have her, no matter what. After all, she was his boss. In a way that bothered him beyond all else. Turning back to his gelding, he knew he should break the awkward silence.

"Are you afraid?" he whispered as he mounted and turned for her response. She looked confused.

"Afraid of what?" she quietly asked. Did he read her eyes and know what she had been thinking? Did he think she was scared of him or was he talking about the killings?

"About being out here with all the killings," Justin replied softly.

As Jesse moved Cozy up beside his gray she let out a sigh of relief. Thank God he couldn't read thoughts.

She whispered, "A little. Do you think there's anybody out here now?" The silence was what was scaring her the most. If Justin would talk, even if it made no sense, she would feel a little better. But she kept quiet. She didn't want to bother him or get them hurt with idle chatter.

Justin smiled. There was that little kid in her again coming out. He liked that side of her. Annie was always so grown up and proper, never any fears or worries. He had never known Annie as much as he thought he did. He figured within a matter of hours he knew more about Jesse than he ever did about Annie.

"I hope not, but we'd better get going. I don't want to be out here past dark." He could tell she was scared, but he had to give her praise for being so quiet and stealthy. Most women would be chattering along behind him, but she just rode in absolute silence. He watched her as she kept her eyes focused on the tree line around them.

They passed through the Forest Service gate and onto open range. They knew they had to watch out doubly for anyone who might want to cause them harm.

Jesse watched as Justin steered his gray east and down toward a grassy slope Jesse knew about. It used to be one of the best places to get maverick cows. Just beyond the slope was a valley with good grass and a large freshwater pond. To the south there was an old cabin she used to stay in when she was a kid, and once or twice when she and Hank were dating.

Jesse urged Cozy up beside Justin. When she was within whispering distance she asked, "Are you thinking they're down towards Gold Water?" He nodded and rode on.

Justin had found dead cows up here in the past and was hoping these cows weren't in such a state. The Gold Water Pond had been a great place to hang out in the past with no one bothering him. But since he found mutilated cows up there he never felt safe there again.

Staying close to the tree line, he maneuvered the gray down a rocky slope, stopped, and listened for a long moment. He heard nothing but magpies singing. That sent up a small red flag in his mind. Magpies were little black and white birds that loved dead animals, however he knew they also liked nuts and bugs, so that didn't mean much. He maneuvered above the clearing on a rocky ledge. From there, one could see the whole meadow just up to the tree line at the end. Beyond that, he knew, was Gold Water Pond.

"Stay here, Jesse. If you hear me yell, go ahead and come down, otherwise stay low, and if you hear any shooting just get on your horse and run for home. Do not slow down till you're safe inside the barn," Justin ordered, and started down the hillside alone. The gray picked his path carefully.

The pond had been named Gold Water Pond for all the gold one old miner supposedly had panned out of the creek that fed into it. The story of Gold Water Meadow told of the very first man who had found it, an old miner named Henry Singer.

He was an easterner who had lost his wife and headed west for gold. His mule, Old Goldie, they say died from exhaustion and dehydration in the meadow and old Henry thought it was his end as well. They say he had been traveling for days, had bypassed all the creeks and the river, and was near death from dehydration.

He lay down next to Old Goldie and planned on dying with her until he saw a buck step from the tree line with water dripping from his mouth. He ran over and found the pond. He named it Gold Water Pond, half for the gold he now sought and mostly for his good friend Old Goldie now lying dead in the meadow. He buried his mule and named the meadow after her as well. Originally it was Old Goldie Meadow, but it has long since been known as just Golden Mule Meadow or Golden Meadow.

The story goes on that Henry built the cabin that still stood, and panned the creek. He pulled color out the very first day and did the same day in and day out for quite a few years. He never associated with people and never staked a claim until one day.

He supposedly hit it rich in a mine tunnel he dug and went to town to stake his claim. In town he staked his claim and headed home. Some bad fellows had overheard him talking to the claim officer, and having seen more gold in Henry's sack than they had ever worked, they followed him home.

They killed Henry and threw his body into Gold Water Pond. The legend says that they never found another speck of gold out of the creek—or the mountain for that fact—and they never found old Henry's mine shaft that he swears was lined with gold just waiting for the taking.

Justin was down the slope and into the meadow before he saw one of the big black birds lift toward the sky from a clump of trees off to his right along the rock hillside. He kicked Badger into a gallop and headed straight for the spot the bird flew from.

Jesse watched in horror as more ravens rose into the sky. That could only mean one thing: something was dead down there. She hoped it wasn't her cows but had a gut feeling it was. That, or worse, maybe a human.

Justin burst into the trees, sending more birds and one lone coyote scattering for safety. He smelled the air and could make out the smell of death hanging heavily in the air. Coppery and pungent, the smell stung his nostrils as he pushed the gray closer.

He searched the ground and followed the smell. It got thicker and stronger. The gray snorted and balked. Justin stepped off and led him through the thick brush. Justin's eyes searched for the cause of the stench. With the smell, it couldn't be the cattle they found missing this morning. Whatever was stinking had been dead a lot longer than a day.

As Justin eased his way through the thick brush, the smell got stronger. Then he could hear the buzz of the blowflies and knew whatever it was had to be hidden within just a few yards.

The brush was so thick he could barely see. He inched along. The thorns clawing at him like fingers reaching out to pull him in. Then he saw it, the mangled carcass of a deer. He breathed a sigh of relief. A noise caught him off guard. He turned and saw a small fawn heading toward Badger, probably thinking he was his mother.

"Whoa, little fellow, he's not your momma. I'd better take care of you. Badger might not like you nuzzling around looking for some milk."

He quickly scooped him up and carried him out of the brush. He couldn't see Jesse from where he was, so swinging up on Badger with the fawn settled under an arm, he headed farther out in the meadow.

* * *

The lone rider laughed as he watched the young man run down the hill to save a dead deer's offspring. He also was intrigued at the young woman who waited alone up on the rocky bench above. She had stepped from her black gelding and sat down, patiently awaiting the return of her hero.

"Not real bright to split up there, sonny. I could sneak in and steal your pretty little woman while you weren't looking, only I might take a few hours to kill her." His strong chest heaved as he chuckled with the delight that would bring him.

The rider watched as the man signaled for the young lady to join him. She mounted and ran down the steep slope to meet up with him. They searched the meadow below him for the lost cows and headed for the pond. He wished he could see their faces when they found their precious cattle, but he knew he had to get back before he was missed.

Killing cattle was a pastime for him. What he really liked was killing women. He liked the way they begged for mercy and cried. Cows just satisfied his cravings over until some poor dumb person wandered his way.

Chapter 6

Justin and Jesse relaxed a little as they headed for the pond. They laughed from the scare they had of thinking they had found their cattle. Their conversation was lighthearted and fun as they reached the pond. Jesse petted the fawn in Justin's arms as they rode side by side.

"What are we going to name him, or is it a her?" Jesse asked. Justin hadn't thought of looking. He reached down and checked.

"It's a boy. And I'm no good at naming things."

"But what about Badger? Who named him?" Jesse asked. She thought the name fit the unsocial gelding to a tee.

"I did. How did you know his name? I didn't think I called him Badger once," Justin questioned.

"I read his nameplate on his stall. He isn't a very social gelding. In fact he's down right unfriendly," Jesse proclaimed.

Justin laughed. "Just like his owner, huh? Maybe he is just hard to get to know. What was it you said? I was like making friends with… oh yeah, a water moccasin."

Jesse defended herself. "I'm sorry, but you aren't very friendly when you meet someone."

They entered the tree line and followed the creek for a hundred yards. Here the trees seemed to open up and give way to the enormous pond. The aspen leaves were green and fluttering in the breeze. The boughs hung over the pond like giant fingers reaching upward toward the heavens.

The shoreline gave way abruptly on the left side, next to a group of bushes. Not far away was a little meadow with lush green grass that looked very enticing to give the horses a quick bite.

Jesse wanted to see how fun Justin really was. She knew they were on serious business, but it was hot and the pond looked cool and refreshing. She knew this time of the year it would be rather cold but she didn't mind, as she longed for a swim.

Jesse wanted to just jump in and forget all her cares and just let them float away on the ripples of the pond. She knew it would be for only maybe a few minutes or so but any minutes away from all her worries would be good ones.

"Justin, do you mind if I go for a swim?" Jesse asked.

A swim? How could she think of such a thing? He was hot, but he wanted to get back to the safety of Running W land.

"Don't you think we should keep moving? It might not be safe."

"I'm so hot, just a quick dip and then we can keep going. Please?" Jesse didn't know why she was asking him but she wanted him to say it was all right.

"I guess it would be all right. I'll take the horses and get them some water," Justin said as he stepped from the gray, placed the fawn on the ground, and reached for Cozy's reins.

Jesse handed him the reins and went to the bushes to remove her jeans and T-shirt.

"Sure you don't want to swim?" Jesse asked as he walked away.

"Positive," he replied. He wanted to swim, but not alone with her, no way could he control the situation in his underwear. He turned his back to her and listened as she gasped when the cold water hit her warm skin.

"You can turn around now, I'm in the water," Jesse revealed as she leaned back and floated out into the pond. Justin turned around and stretched out on the ground, watching her float around. She looked so relaxed and at peace, he couldn't take his eyes off her.

The fawn wandered over and nuzzled around him looking for milk.

"It won't be too long before we get you back and get you some good mare's milk, that should make you grow big." Justin petted the fawn and soon he stretched out beside him and fell asleep in the grass.

"Hey Justin?" Jesse called.

"What?" Justin replied.

"Who's Karla? Is she your girlfriend? What does she think about you and me riding together?" Jesse hadn't meant to ask, it just seemed funny not to know.

Justin smiled. "You're a little know-it-all, aren't you? Karla is nothing to me. She wants to be my girlfriend but she's a little too good for me."

"Too good? What's that mean?" Jesse asked without thinking.

"It means I'm not good enough for her," Justin explained with a grunt that warned Jesse not to ask any more questions. She ignored it.

"That sounds to me like a dumb way for a man to say he doesn't like you. Why don't you let her decide who's not good enough for her? Obviously she likes you, so she must think you're okay." Justin was a lot more complicated than Hank had ever even dreamed about being. Hank was more into the willingness to spread one's legs for him. He didn't care about right or wrong, just willing.

"Are you trying to give me dating advice?" Justin responded. Logan had told him some about her husband last night and it wasn't real impressive.

"No, not at all. It's just you seem so nice. I'm wondering why you're single. You're not too bad looking as far as anybody around here goes. Seems to me girls would be knocking down the gates to get to you. Don't you want a girlfriend?"

"Where's your husband?" Justin sounded hurt.

Jesse stopped floating and looked at him momentarily. He lay stretched out holding the two horses that munched grass around him and stroking the fawn that lay sleeping as if his world hadn't fallen apart. He looked so handsome and strong, all but his face, which was twisted into a frown.

"I'm sorry, Justin. I didn't mean to bring up painful memories. My husband is a whole other story," she said as she leaned back and drifted out into the center of the pond.

"He wasn't sure what a marriage really consisted of and now he will never know. Soon I'll be rid of him for good."

Justin looked at her and waited for her to explain more.

"I found him in bed with another woman. That same day, I packed up and moved back here without a word to him." Jesse knew her voice was giving away all her feelings, but she just stared up through the canopy of aspen branches overhead, wishing that tears didn't well up in her eyes to give away how she really felt about Hank's betrayal.

"Well, I'm sure it will work out for you, Jess. At least you made it through the wedding and nine years before he turned out to be an ass."

Maybe Jesse's book wasn't so far off. Maybe Justin only loved with half a heart. She wanted to ask about the woman who broke his heart, but knew she had better stop questioning him for one day.

"Hurry up, Jess, we'd better get going," Justin yelled. "This fawn needs some milk."

"All right, I'll head for shore." Jesse dove under and swam toward shore. The water was murky and hard to see through, but it felt cool and crisp against her skin and that was all that counted.

Suddenly she bumped into something hard below the surface, and it stopped her. Whatever it was, it was quite large. She opened her eyes and saw it, a face looking at her under the water. Not just any face, but a cow's face; its eyes were huge and buggy. It looked as though it were in pain.

She screamed but realized she was underwater, and she was horrified by the gulp of water she swallowed. She shot up and screamed. Justin was to his feet and in the water before she could explain.

She tried to swim away from the cow but her foot was tangled in what felt like a rope. She yelled in fear and tried to pull free, but her ankle hurt and whatever was around it was getting tighter.

Justin's arms circled her. "What's wrong, Jess?"

"My foot is caught in a rope!" Jesse screamed as she went under again and struggled to free herself. Justin pulled her to the surface.

"A rope?" Justin questioned as he held on to her.

"It's hooked to a dead cow!" Jesse panicked and went under again as Justin dove under and started to cut the rope around her ankle. Jesse was fighting to stay above water. It was no use—he couldn't get ahold of the rope with Jesse fighting like she was. He had to get her to calm down, even though he knew if the roles were reversed he would hate it as much as she did.

Justin came back to the surface and grabbed Jesse by the waist. "Jess, look at me!" Jesse tried to get her bearings straight but still she thrashed around. "Look at me now!" Justin yelled.

She looked at him, her eyes filled with fear and panic. Justin could tell she thought she was dying, but she needed to calm down or he could accidentally cut her while trying to free her.

"Look into my eyes." She did as she was told. "Good, now you have to calm down. I don't want to cut you with my knife. I'm going down one more time and then I will help you to shore."

Jesse mumbled, "Okay."

Justin went under again and cut the rope. In an instant she was free. With an arm around her waist Justin swam her to shore. Jesse sank and sat there shaking. She didn't feel well, and suddenly she felt like a child alone with nobody to run to. She curled up her knees and, placing her head on them, shivered from the picture in her mind of the poor cow.

Justin grabbed her clothes and sat down next to her. He wrapped an arm around her shoulders and pulled her close to him. She sank into his warmth and felt her eyes filling up with tears. He felt so warm and welcoming. Jesse turned her head into his shoulder and sobbed.

Justin hadn't wanted to hold her so tight but it felt right. She had been through a scary ordeal and he could feel her body quake as she sobbed into his shoulder. His heart lurched as she wrapped her arms around his neck and clung to him.

He picked her up and moved to the grass by the horses. As he sat he pulled her across his lap, her arms still around his neck. Her face now nuzzled into his neck, she still sobbed uncontrollably. He held her for what seemed like hours. The longer he held her the harder it was for him to remember she was scared and not his to be had.

After a while the tears stopped and she still never moved, but he was enjoying her closeness too much to want it to end. He could feel her every curve against him; the beating of her heart made his blood pump and the thin breath of air that stirred his neck from her breathing was enough to drive him mad.

Suddenly Jesse looked up into his eyes. Her face was red, and her eyes were swollen from crying. He watched her lower lip quake like a sad lost child and that was his undoing.

He lowered his head and pressed his lips to hers. She tasted sweet and tempting. His lips brushed hers in airy bliss. He pulled his lips away as if he had never kissed her at all and looked down at her face. Her eyes showed nothing but pleasure; her mouth parted ever so slightly waiting for another kiss. Justin smiled to himself as he lowered his head to, once again, claim her lips.

This time wasn't so gentle. His hunger and passion came into play. He kissed her hard and demandingly as if she were the last woman he would ever kiss. She matched his need and hunger with as much passion as she had in her.

Her mouth parted as he slipped his tongue between her lips. His kisses were savage and unyielding. Jesse met every savage kiss with one of her own. Tingling spasms ran down her spine, making her skin sensitive to every touch of his mouth and hands.

His hands explored her soft velvety back down to her waist, and he cupped her firm bottom and pulled her closer to his growing manhood. Only the layers of his clothing and her undergarments kept them apart. He wanted to strip down and dive into her until the break of day.

Justin slid his hand down off one shoulder, taking with it her bra strap and cupped a soft breast. Jesse's sudden breath was stolen by his kiss, which left her breathless gain. Justin rubbed her nipple until it was hard and taut. His mouth left hers to scatter kisses down her neck and tease her rock hard nipple with a few flicks of his tongue. Jesse tossed her head back and moaned in pleasure.

Justin gave the other breast the same attention before abandoning them for the sweet taste of her lips again.

They kissed like they were starving for one another. Jesse ran her hands down his back and across his chest. Her hands left tingling trails in their wake. Justin was quickly losing all of his senses. He knew making love to her would be the only thing to relieve the burning in his gut.

Jesse leaned closer into him and straddled his waist. She could feel his engorged manhood and knew what he wanted. His kisses sent more shivers up her spine. Only layers of clothing separated them from the release they both wanted so badly.

Justin's kisses trailed down her neck and over her shoulders. He laid her on her back and trailed kisses down over her belly and up to her breast again. He took one soft, rosy nipple into his mouth. Jesse moaned in pleasure. He sucked and licked until she thought she could not stand it any longer.

He moved his attention to the other breast and was happy to catch it up on the attention. Jesse moaned and ran her hands down to the top of his pants. A deep throaty sound escaped him as she undid his pants and slid her hand into his pants and stroked his growing manhood.

Justin could stand it no longer, he wanted her right here and now. He scattered kisses down her belly and down the inside of her thighs. Jesse moaned and raised her hips towards him in an inviting movement.

The cow was forgotten as they sat entangled on the shoreline. Their bodies were on fire from each other's touch and lending promise to each other for satisfaction.

The ring of a gunshot and the unmistakable smack of the bullet off the tree above their heads sent them both back to their senses. Justin jumped up and threw Jesse's clothes at her.

"I never thought I would ever tell a woman this, but get dressed quick, we have to go now." Justin snatched up the fawn and the reins while Jesse quickly dressed. Handing Cozy's reins to Jesse, he took one last look at the woman who he knew he would never hold again. Her face and her inviting body would always be in his dreams, but never in his arms again, he knew that much to be truth.

"Get on and ride, and don't look back!" Justin yelled.

Jesse nodded and they were mounted and running toward the ranch in a matter of minutes. Jesse and Justin both knew the shot was a warning shot meant for them. They ran the distance back to the gate, raced through, and were back to the ranch by eight o'clock.

* * *

The man on the bay smiled as he placed his gun back in the scabbard. They turned a great scare into a screwfest in a matter of minutes. He would be the one to calm the next screams that young woman would have. He smiled as he mounted and watched them run for home. And thought, "Now I really must be getting back."

He turned the bay toward his home and sunk his spurs into it. The bay snorted and obeyed the big man whose heart was like ice.

Chapter 7

Once inside the safety of the breezeway Jesse dismounted and collapsed on the floor beside Cozy.

"You okay, Jess?"

"Yes, I guess so. I just have a lot to take in for an afternoon, with the cow and then that shot." Jesse's face flushed and Justin knew what else she was thinking of.

Justin smiled and kept his distance. He couldn't have that happen again. Who knows how far it might have gone had they not been interrupted?

"Hey, Justin, do you think someone was watching us and saw what we were doing?" She paused, thinking about what they were doing. She was embarrassed at the fact that they were so brazen about their kissing and fondling.

Smiling, Justin watched her face as it turned red.

"Yeah, I think they were watching us. I'm not sure how much they saw. Your face is getting a little red. Are you blushing?" he asked as he helped the fawn into one of the stalls.

"Yes, I guess I am. I've never kissed in public and I'm a little uncomfortable with the idea of what we were doing up there," Jesse explained as she faced the ground.

Justin was momentarily dumbfounded.

"You're a married woman. How could you never have kissed in public? What about your wedding? I think the kissing was the least of what we were doing, Jess."

"Hank and I, we... never... I mean, we eloped, and I don't want to talk about what we were doing up there. Just please let's make sure it never happens again." She stood erect and jerked the saddle from Cozy's back. Justin led Badger to his stall and did the same. He watched as she slumped against the wall and sank into the straw and could tell she had had a little too much for one day.

He didn't dare get close to her or try to support her. She might cry or turn and look at him with those big eyes, and that would be hazardous for both of them. So he did the next best thing—he went on with his evening chores and figured he would check on her just before he left to make sure she was okay.

Jesse waited until Justin had moved down to Badger's stall before collapsing in a frenzy of emotions. She pulled the stall door shut and curled up in the straw. The poor cow's face floated across her mind. She cringed and tried to remember something pleasant. What came to her mind was Justin's kisses, his warm hands burning her flesh as he stroked her back. She drifted away in her thoughts and must have fallen asleep. All she remembered hearing was Justin's voice telling her everything was all right as he carried her to her bedroom and set her down under the covers.

Jesse opened her eyes and looked up to find him staring back at her. He was a handsome man, definitely too good to be true.

"Shhh, you're all right, you fell asleep in Cozy's stall so I carried you up to your room. I'll take off your boots and your cap and let you get some sleep. You had a hard day and deserve a good night's sleep." She nodded and rolled over on her side.

She listened to him talk nonchalantly about this and that as he pulled off her boots and socks. He then reached behind her neck, undid her hat, and removed it. She wasn't sure it happened but she could have sworn she felt his hands undo her braid and let her hair loose.

Justin watched as her breath evened out into sleep, and pulled the covers up to her chin. She was so pretty when she slept. Her brow had no worry line and she looked like she had not a care in the world. If he were a loving man he would curl up beside her and never leave her side.

Justin stepped from her room and stopped by the kitchen to use her phone. He knew he had to call the police to report the shot and the cows. As he dialed the number he wished he had never taken her with him today. She could have been killed and then what would he have done, lived the rest of his life with that regret as well? She had been there three days and had almost gotten shot twice—not very good odds.

The deputy answered. Justin quickly explained what had happened and who was with him. The deputy informed him that it was too late to do anything about it tonight but he would send the sheriff out first thing in the morning.

After hanging up the phone Justin poured himself a cold cup of coffee, heated it in the microwave, and sat at Jesse's table. He looked around and realized for the first time how clean and tidy the house was. She had put a lot of work into it.

New little black and white cows lined the windowsill. He laughed as he picked one up and read the bottom of it. "Love's First Kiss." Another read, "He Was A Hero." Justin was going to have to ask the reason for these cows.

Tomorrow he would have to show the sheriff around most of the morning, which should keep him from running into her, anything to stay away from her. He had proven to himself he had no willpower against her already and he sure as hell didn't need a repeat of today's little show happening again anytime soon. If it hadn't been for that shot he knew exactly how far their little episode would have went. He would have had a lot more to apologize for than just kissing and stroking her skin.

Chapter 8

The next morning Jesse stayed in the house until she saw Justin and the sheriff leave, then she made a quick run for her truck. She would spend most of the day in town, at the store. That should keep Justin away from her and her away from him.

It was Wednesday and the store was crowded as people roamed up and down the aisles. Molly taught her how to run the cash register and how to ring up merchandise. She made a few mistakes, charged a few people too much and felt bad about it after she realized her mistake. They didn't seem to care but she swore she would pay them back the next time they came in.

She watched everybody warily to see what kind of people they were. Most of the customers were normal people like her, but as soon as one of the other kind came in everybody would be quiet and walk to the other side of the store.

Molly warned Jesse not to treat them any differently, just smile, say hello, thank you, and goodbye. Jesse liked working with Molly. She met Gus a time or two. He was a short fat man who worked in the back, kept to himself, and never said much to anyone.

Jesse wasn't sure she trusted him a hundred percent but he was a good, hard worker. Molly and Jesse worked shoulder to shoulder all day. At closing time they walked each other to their trucks and left for home.

Jesse knew this was a good profitable business. The best part was that her day flew by quickly and she never had time to think about Justin. She wanted to know what he had found out with the sheriff and was eager to talk to Logan about what the results were.

When she pulled up to the house she saw Justin's pickup, Mary's van, and a little blue car she had never seen before.

As she walked in the front door she froze. Logan and Mary were sitting in their normal spots at the head of the table, Justin to the right. Beside him was a very pretty giggling blonde who seemed to be hanging on his every word and his arm.

"Hi," Logan said as Mary got up and handed her a plate.

"Hard day at the store?" Justin never lifted his head.

"Yes, I guess you could say that, it sure was busy," Jesse replied. "How did everything go around here? What did the sheriff say?" she asked as she took her place across the table from Justin.

Logan could tell there was something going on between Justin and Jesse. He had known both of them for a long time and knew without a doubt that some tension was between them. About what he hadn't a clue, but he knew for sure it was there.

"Oh, he said the cow was dead and that he would make a report," Justin replied with a mouth full of mashed potatoes.

"That's it, the cow is dead? What about the shot, what did he say about that?" Jesse was pissed and her voice was rising rapidly. The stupid sheriff wouldn't know a dead cow from a live one and he sure as hell had never been shot at or he would be out finding the idiot who had tried to kill them.

Justin looked up into Jesse's eyes. He could tell it was more than the cow or the shot that had her jumping. It was Karla and he knew it.

"Who are you?" Jesse asked as she glared at Karla.

"Oh, I'm Karla," said the girl in an almost non-existent voice with a fake southern drawl.

"Karla what? Do you have a last name, Karla?" Jesse asked in an authoritative tone.

"Jenson. You must be Jessica Walker. I heard in town you were back." Karla felt her way in the dark to see how friendly Jesse was. "How long are you staying?"

"Forever," Jesse angrily replied.

"Oh, well, welcome back home then."

Justin looked up again at Jesse and saw hurt and anger in her eyes along with a confused look he couldn't quite understand. He didn't want to hurt her at all but Karla always just showed up whenever and stayed. He tried to get her to move away from him but it didn't work well with her, she was just a very clingy person.

Jesse began to shovel mashed potatoes into her mouth, followed by green beans and chicken. She was starving but she didn't want to stay around Justin and Karla any more than need be. Besides, they had not waited on her for dinner, judging by Justin's plate.

Jesse couldn't believe it. They had almost made love up at the pond had someone not tried to scare them. Who knows what might have happened, and now he sits at the table with a blond bimbo holding onto his arm. It was like looking at a younger version of Hank.

She had to get out of the house before she screamed at him. She knew she had no right to tell him who he could or couldn't love even though he had said she wasn't for him. Now he looked like maybe he changed his mind.

Mary and Logan looked back and forth between Justin staring down at his plate and Jesse inhaling her food and wondered what had happened while they were gone yesterday.

"May I be excused?" Jesse said before she realized she didn't have to say that in her own house. "I'm going to go out and feed Cozy and Boe." With that she strode outside to the barn. "The nerve of that bastard bringing his girlfriends here after yesterday."

She fed and watered her horses and when she could find nothing else to keep her from the ranch house she turned and headed back. She could hear Karla laughing from across the driveway.

Jesse circled the house and climbed the old oak tree to the second floor. She wanted nothing to do with Karla or Justin right now or ever again. Once through the window she relaxed and sank down in her oversized chair to read a few more pages of her book.

Tonight it was Colette, and how she wanted it so bad she said it in her every movement. The whore, slut, bitch, and whatever else she could think of. He gave her what she begged for and rolled over and escaped into another woman's arms.

"Grr, I'm so tired of assholes. When will a real man come along who just wants me and me only? Is that so much to ask for?"

As she tossed the torn man and his newfound slut to the floor, Jesse listened as the voices faded downstairs. Her face pink with anger, she muttered, "Go ahead, Justin. She wants it, go give it to her. Asshole."

She hated herself for sounding so spoiled. She was still a married woman, at least until those papers came back. She would head into Republic tomorrow first thing and see a lawyer about making her a single woman forever.

The phone rang. She picked it up. It was Jack.

"Jack, how are you?" Jesse asked.

"Good. I just heard over the scanner someone shot at you. Are you okay? Do you want me to come over and see you? I could make you some tea or soup," Jack asked.

He sounded so sweet. Jesse wanted to say yes just so that she could rub it into Justin's face that she too could find someone else.

Jesse had an idea. She wasn't sure she was up to it, but, oh well. "Can we go out to the bar and go dancing tonight?"

"Sure, I'll pick you up in a half an hour." Jack sounded so happy. "Will that be enough time for you to get ready?"

"That'll be great. See you then," Jesse exclaimed, and hung up so that she could jump in the shower and get dressed for a long night of dancing.

After dressing and applying some makeup she headed downstairs. Logan, Mary, Justin, and Karla were sitting around the kitchen all chatting happily when she entered.

Logan let out a shrill whistle as he saw her.

"Holy cow, Jessica, you look great. Where are you going?" Jesse had let down her hair, one thing she rarely ever did.

"I've got a date. I'm going dancing with Jack," Jesse explained. Justin spun around and looked her square in the eye.

"Where are you two heading?" Justin asked.

"The Old Crow," Jesse answered.

The Old Crow was a cowboy bar that hopped all night long. A lot of young couples used to go there to dance the night away, then end up at the Crow's Nest Motel right next door for the night.

Karla squealed in delight. "Oh, how fun."

Jesse saw a strange smirk come over Justin's face. "Would you like to run out there tonight too, Karla?"

Jesse was mad enough to spit. Mary jumped up and hugged Jesse. "Oh, how fun, I wish I were going too. I love to dance."

Logan winked and nodded to Jesse.

"Mary, we could run out for a couple hours too, if the kids don't mind."

Jesse was only too eager to reply. "Not at all, come along."

Jack showed up and was surprised to be greeted by a caravan of people. Jesse opened the passenger door and was about to slide into the seat of Jack's truck. She was surprised and outraged at the sudden presence of Justin behind her.

"Hey, you don't mind if we ride with you, do you? Good." Without giving Jack or Jesse time to answer he pushed Karla across the seat next to Jack, then pushed Jesse in and slid in next to her.

"Why aren't you driving yourself, Justin?" Jesse questioned.

Justin had practically begged Logan to drive his minivan so that they could all ride back with them. He didn't want to let Jesse and Jack to have the chance to be alone.

"Well, Logan said in case we drink tonight we had all better ride home with him. Karla lives just down the road from Jack and he could give her a lift home. And Jesse and I will ride home with Mary and Logan." Justin had it all planned out.

"Oh, I would probably be able to give Jesse a ride home," Jack said. He was hoping to get Jesse drunk and have to stay at the Crow's Nest Motel. He hadn't liked Justin very much for quite a while and didn't like him at all now.

Jack had been hitting on a barmaid up at the Circle D Saloon when it got a little out of hand. Justin had stepped in on her behalf and broke Jack's jaw, so Jack owed him one. And with a few drinks tonight he might just get it if he wasn't careful.

The drive was a long one with Justin's arm in her side. He moved it once but he put it behind her, and that was dangerous as it brought back all the memories of the pond. Her face felt flushed as she thought about it. She felt Justin's eyes on her. He must have been thinking the same thing, for he slid his arm back down to his side.

"Sorry, Jesse."

"It's okay, Justin."

Karla and Jack didn't miss a move or a comment that happened between Justin and Jesse. They kept their eyes on the ones they came with and both were planning on taking them home as well.

Karla chatted about this and that although nothing made much sense. Jesse wasn't sure what Justin saw in her. She was pretty enough, but her mind had long since left her.

Jack sat in silence. He was still trying to figure out how the hell he had gotten stuck next to Karla and not Jesse. He noticed Justin and Jesse never looked at one another, and when they did, Jesse's cheeks would flush.

He could tell the look—it was lust, a pure raw drive for sex. He wanted to see it in Jesse's eyes when she looked at him, not the poor dumb cowboy who had to defend every woman who was done wrong. Jack was conceiving a plan as he drove with the annoying Karla chattering beside him. He knew just what would send Jesse running to save him, and send Justin the poor dumb cowboy soaring right out of her mind.

He was going to have to make a few calls when they got to the bar, as he had to have some good witnesses on hand, and a few good friends.

He knew how much Jesse used to hate violence. If he could provoke Justin into hitting him, then Jesse would come to his rescue and turn her hatred onto Justin. She might even fire him. That would suit Jack just fine.

He might be able to even talk her into staying at the Crow's Nest Motel with him because, of course, he will have had too much to drink and so will she. And with neither one of them able to drive home, one thing would be sure to lead to another.

He figured he should be able to get a good screw out of her if he stood his ground during the punch and she saw what kind of a man he really was. He smiled to himself. He wanted her so badly he could taste it.

His friends had ridiculed him when he let Hank waltz in and steal her right out from under his covers even though she had never let him under there with her, but his friends hadn't known that. He was going to show them all, and Justin, too. He hated him; he was a jerk and a wannabe hero. Well, let him try to save her from him after tonight.

The conversation droned on, mostly on Karla's part. Jesse wished she could toss her out the window. She wished she had thought to ride with Logan and Mary or drive herself. Only then Justin probably would have figured something out to ride with her, saying she wasn't safe alone, or at least without him.

He was the one who was giving her the cold shoulder at the house. Why did he seem to care so much right now? He was acting like a jealous boyfriend. She turned and looked at his face. That was exactly how he was acting. Did he really care for her? If he did, then why did he keep pushing her away? Why did he bring Karla to the house?

Justin turned and looked into the same curious big eyes he had seen two days ago up on the fence line. Jesse looked at him like he was a foreign creature that she wished she could dissect and figure out what made it tick.

He hated to act like the jealous husband figure, but he didn't want her hanging out with Jack. He didn't trust him or his friends and refused to let her get hurt by him in any way. Maybe he was just protecting his boss. Yeah, right. Who was he kidding? She hadn't even come close to barking an order since he met her, at him or anybody else.

A part of him wanted to turn around and go back home and sleep, but the other part of him, the part that seemed to be ruling his thoughts, wanted to go along and make sure Jesse didn't sleep with Jack.

If she was going to sleep with anyone, it was going to be him. He knew, given the chance, he was going to finish what they started up at the pond.

Chapter 9

The Old Crow was packed when they strolled through the swinging doors. Karla hung on Justin's arm, her face showing her pleasure of being there with him in tow.

Jack offered his arm to Jesse but she just ignored it and followed Justin and Karla in and up to the bar to order drinks. Logan and Mary ambled in soon after and made their way toward an empty table in the back corner.

"Jesse, what do you want to drink?" Justin asked.

"A Pepsi, please."

"A Pepsi? No, get her a shot, let's get this party started," Jack chimed in.

"No, please, just a soda is fine. I don't feel like drinking." Jesse had never been much of a drinker. People did stupid things when they drank and she had lived ten years with the perfect example of that.

When Hank was intoxicated he slept around, got into fights, and rode unrideable bulls. She had watched in fear as he would fight bigger, tougher men or climb on a "widow maker" bull. The worst was when she would spend a sleepless night waiting for him to return from another woman's bed.

Jack ordered a whiskey on the rocks and Karla ordered some fruity foo-foo drink. Jesse figured it fit her to a tee. She listened to see what Justin would order.

"Two Coors Lights and an iced tea," Justin ordered. He had to agree with Jesse on one thing; drinking was not much fun, especially in the morning. He paid for their drinks and carried the beers over for Logan and Mary.

Jesse smiled when Justin placed the two beers in front of them. She had been sure he was drinking one of them. He surprised her yet again by taking the iced tea.

They talked and listened to the music for about half an hour. Jack invited her to dance almost every dance but when she refused he would grab Karla and swing her around the dance floor.

Logan and Mary climbed from the booth when a slow song came on and helped fill the dance floor. Karla and Jack danced into the corner. Jesse could see they were beginning to like each other. Their dancing got closer and closer until their bodies were practically rubbing up against each other. Jesse was pleased, as she really wasn't romantically interested in Jack.

"I'm sorry you're not getting to dance with Karla," Jesse whispered to Justin, not really sorry at all.

"Oh, that's all right. I'm sorry you haven't felt like dancing with Romeo all night." Justin snorted. He hadn't meant to sound so mean, it just came out.

"Why are you being so mean to me? I was trying to talk to you, not pick a fight." Jesse was hurt by the tone in his voice. She had hoped they could forget the scene by the pond and be friends.

Justin knew the best thing to do would be to not apologize and just let her be mad at him, but he hated to see the hurt in her eyes. She hadn't done anything wrong but follow her gut instinct and his lead.

"Jesse, I'm sorry for snapping at you. Do you want to dance?"

"Yes, I'd like to." They stood and walked to the edge of the dance floor. The slow song was soon forgotten as Justin put an arm around her waist and held her right hand and pulled her close to him.

She could feel his breath on her neck and she longed to lean closer to him. She could feel his pulse in his fingers. As he held her hand, she wondered if he could feel hers as well.

They swayed with the music and even though they saw no one else in the room, everybody else saw them. Jesse moved in a little closer, her cheek almost touched his chest, and with a quick step Justin made sure it did touch and stayed there.

Jack's temperature rose as he looked over and saw Jesse and Justin as close as they could get, then looked to the sidelines where his buddies sat. They giggled and laughed when they saw him lose again to a cowboy.

Jesse looked up into Justin's blue eyes and saw confusion staring back. "What are you so confused about, Justin?"

"Why are you here with me? I'm not rich or famous that you know of. So why? What do you want from me?" Justin had to know what she thought. Where she thought all of this affection was going to lead to.

"I don't know what I want."

"Well I know what I want. And I'm sure of it." He stepped back as the music ended. He wanted her for a night, maybe two, but not forever.

"Are you?" Jesse smiled as she asked.

Suddenly taken aback, Justin couldn't figure out what she was asking. Was he sure what he wanted? Yes, very sure.

"Am I what?"

"Rich or famous?"

"Would it make any difference?" Justin asked. She was already turning into Annie. Money, do you have money? Maybe that was what she should really be asking.

"Probably not, just curious. The way you said it was as if you might be rich and or famous."

"What if I were rich and famous?" Justin wondered what she would do if she learned he had well over a million in his bank account.

"Well, I had famous and am not interested in that at all, and I have my own money so I'm not interested in your money either. So if you're rich and famous why are you working on my ranch?" Jesse had seen enough spoiled rich boys to last a lifetime, and the famous ones had no loyalty.

"For the view." Justin was looking right at her, and she felt her cheeks flush. Jesse knew where this conversation was leading. Next door to the Crow's Nest. She had to change the conversation quickly.

"Hey, Justin, I'm tired and I really don't want to go home with Jack at all. Do you think we could get Logan and Mary and sneak out without having to confront Jack or Karla?"

"That's funny, I was just thinking the same thing about Karla." They both laughed.

"What do you think?" Jesse asked again.

"Maybe, I'll see." Justin knew how Jesse felt; he felt the same way. He ambled over to Logan and whispered in his ear. Jesse watched as Logan nodded and he and Mary got up and walked out. Justin walked toward the door, signaled her to follow, and she did.

Once outside they both ran for the van and dove inside the open side door like they had just robbed the place.

"Drive!" Justin yelled in a comical tone.

"Where shall I take you, young man?" Logan teased as he started the car and headed for home. Jesse loved the teasing and joking that went on between Mary, Logan, and Justin.

She was laughing out loud when Justin placed his hand on her head and eased it back down to the floor.

"Out of here, now! Don't worry, madam, I won't let them kill you while I'm alive, just keep your head down."

They all laughed when Jesse used her most pitiful voice and replied, "Oh, my big strong man, you make me feel so safe."

"Yes, he's known for that. He is Sheriff Justin, the biggest, strongest, feel-safest man on this here range, Missy," Mary added.

Jesse was sorry to see the game come to an end. She smiled in the darkness and touched Justin's hand. He turned and looked her way as though he could make out every detail of her face. His hand unfolded and he grasped her hand in his all the way home to the Running W.

Logan and Mary dropped them off in front of her house where Justin's truck was parked. Jesse turned and headed for the house.

"Is that it?" Justin asked.

"Is what it?" Jesse responded.

"I get to hold your hand but I don't get to kiss you goodnight?" Justin knew he shouldn't, but he couldn't go home without seeing that cute little look on her face as he teased her about it.

She blushed. "No, you can't kiss me goodnight. The last kiss didn't stop there, and I have to file for my divorce tomorrow. So I need my rest."

Justin teased a little farther to watch the red tinge from her flushed face drop to her throat. "Then you'll be a single woman. Who will you chase after then, Jack?"

"Why do you think I want to chase after anyone, as you so kindly put it?"

"A woman like you can't be single too long, you're too good looking." Justin's own words were pissing him off but he knew they were true. Jesse wouldn't be single for very long after her divorce was finalized.

"Thanks for the compliment, but I'm not interested in marriage," Jesse replied without hesitation.

"You're not?"

"I had a great teacher who taught me what hell was. But what I'm wondering about is why you're not married, Justin. Karla seems to like you. What about her?" she teased.

"Karla is a little much for me. Someday when we have more time I'll tell you all about me and my love life."

"Promise? I would invite you in for a cup of coffee if you aren't sleepy, but you have to keep your distance."

"If I have to keep my distance then I'll go home. Goodnight, Jesse."

"Goodnight, Justin. I'll see you tomorrow."

Jesse watched as the lights from a truck drove up her driveway. Who could be here this time of night? The truck stopped and Jesse could tell it was Karla. She quickly exited and went to Justin.

"Hey, you left me," she exclaimed. She was obviously drunk.

Jesse wanted to stay and watch Justin defend himself, but she was tired and knew he would soon send her away. She turned and walked inside. Once upstairs she crept down the dark hallway and peeked out the south window to see what they were up to.

She was shocked to see them locked in an embracing kiss; she gasped and refused to look at them again.

"Why, that bastard! He just wanted to come up with me tonight to my bed and now he's down there kissing her. Well I hope she has a waterbed and you drown. Jerk!" As she moved from the window, her temper rose. "I hope he dies from suffocation while he's locked onto her lips."

Jesse covered the distance to her room and sunk down in her bed. She was horrified that he could do that out in front of her house, with her inside. Heck, he probably wouldn't have cared if she were still standing out on the front porch watching.

She heard a pickup start up and drive off. Just one pickup drove off, meaning Karla had gone home with Justin.

He was starting to act a lot like the man in her book—a different woman every night, and a couple tonight. Maybe he should write a new book: *Loving With Only a Quarter of Your Heart*, or in Justin's case, *That Cold Icy Thing in Your Chest that Doesn't Beat.*

"A bastard. That's what he is. I can see a future with him would be the same as a future with Hank—nonexistent."

Jesse vowed she would never speak to him again, or get in his way around the ranch doing what he did best. She would think about telling him she didn't ever want to see him again. Except she liked the way he worked.

She couldn't help but think about yesterday by the pond after she had seen the cow. He was so kind and caring, and then so passionate as if he had been wanting to kiss her forever. As if he had been yearning to do it.

He was the only man who made her believe in romance novels, and he had just become off limits for everything.

Jesse fell asleep dreaming of Justin's kisses, and much, much more.

Chapter 10

The next morning bright and early Jesse woke up, dressed, got in her truck, and headed for Republic. She had promised Molly she would stop by later and help at the store.

Last night, she had let herself get caught up in the moment... again. She had to stop getting so close to Justin. He was dangerous, and with him she lacked her willpower. She decided she would have to spend more time at the store, or with Jack. That was the only way she was going to keep herself sane.

For today and tomorrow she had to keep away from Justin. After that, Marnie would be here and then they could spend the weekend together. She couldn't wait to see her again. She loved Marnie and wanted the company she would bring. Jesse had always been able to tell Marnie anything.

Republic was the same as she remembered it. It was a lot bigger than Danville, almost seven or eight times the size, but still had a small-town atmosphere.

All the buildings looked authentic to an 1880s mining town. Log buildings with antique front arches and signs bearing The Prospector, The Golden Nugget, and Strike It Rich Saloon were up and down the street. Horses hitched to a rail out behind the building showed the laid-back, old-time mentality of a few of the folks around.

Jesse laughed as she read a sign out in front of a store: "Horses in the back, Mustangs in the front."

Jesse went straight to the lawyer's office. A long time ago the building used to be the claims office. She loved the old folklore and legends every building, creek, or hole in the ground seemed to have around here.

The door was unlocked, and as she stepped in, a bell on the door chimed her arrival. She looked around the small office. The inside smelled of paint, and by the fresh look of the place she could tell it had recently seen a fresh coat. She couldn't say much for the color they had chosen. The whole place looked like the inside of a fish, with a dark pink paint covering every inch of the walls.

In a strange way it made her think of all those days when she was a child and spent time fishing with her grandpa down at Dead Man's Hole on the river, which got its name after a man had drowned there. How she wished she could go fishing right then, just drop all her cares, grab a pole and go. If only her grandpa was still alive to take her. She could sit on the bank and watch as he baited her hook; she hated to touch the slimy little crawdads.

A large desk filled up the front, leaving a small area for waiting. A bookcase with an abundant amount of books covered one wall. Jesse was nervous. Hank wasn't going to like it that she hired her own lawyer or that she filed for a divorce without telling him first.

In fact, she knew he might come looking for her or try to take her back with him to Caldwell. She knew what she had to do—get rid of his ties to her forever. The ring was the first thing she gave up, then all his memories that seemed to haunt her every move.

She had slipped the ring from her finger as soon as she had walked from the bedroom after seeing Hank and that blond bimbo together. She hadn't tossed it like she had at first wanted to do; instead she just dropped it inside her jewelry box as a reminder to never trust another man.

A short chubby man came out of the back room with a rag and a bottle of Windex. He had a pleasant look about him. His eyes twinkled and his mouth had small lines around the edges of them, which made Jesse think he probably laughed a lot.

"How may I help you?" he asked without slowing down in his pursuit of the dirty window. He sprayed and scrubbed as Jesse thought about how to tell him what she needed.

"I need a lawyer," Jesse blurted out.

The man stopped cleaning and looked at her quizzically.

"Are you in some kind of trouble, young lady?" he asked as though she were six years old and had just come running into his shop with a stolen sucker.

"No, I'm not in trouble. At least I don't think I am."

"I am a lawyer, but I do mostly divorces and family problems. As well as clean the windows." He laughed at his own joke.

"Good. I need a divorce."

Jesse found herself sounding like an idiot. Her needs were short and easily put into words, however she found she wasn't sounding much like she regretted her decision.

"Okay. My name is Tom Geller, and I think, or hope, I can help you. Tell me your story from the beginning. Please sit down; you're making me nervous with all your fidgeting around."

Jesse hadn't realized she had been fidgeting, but then realized her hands were white from nervously wringing them together. She let out a long breath she had been holding and tried to relax.

Tom set the rag and bottle down and came over to the desk and sat opposite her, behind the large wood desk.

Jesse sat down in the large fluffy chair and told her whole story. Tom listened with anxious ears.

"Has he ever hit or kicked you?" Tom asked when Jesse had finished her story.

"Yes, he hit me twice, but he said it was an accident," Jesse explained to Tom. She sounded more like she was defending him yet again.

"Honey, they all say that. I think I can help you right away. I need his address and fifty dollars."

He grabbed a piece of paper from the cabinet behind him and started writing.

"Sign right here and here, please," he said as he pointed to a couple places on a piece of paper. She did as she was told.

"Good," he said after she had dished out fifty dollars.

"Now what?" Jesse asked, curious as to what a divorce actually entailed.

"Now we send him the papers, wait for him to sign, and then, honey, you are officially divorced. It's that easy. He hit you, so we can skip everything else and get a restraining order against him so he can't come close to you. In doing so, we hurry up the divorce process by two months, which means in two weeks you, young lady, should be a free woman."

"Sounds great."

"Only if that's what you want."

"It is."

"Have a great day then and don't worry, he can't hurt you anymore."

"So, I can leave now?" Jesse was amazed at how quick a divorce really was. It took her forever to get married and realize that she wanted, or needed, a divorce. Now, in ten minutes, she had ended it all.

"Yes. But I'll need to see you when I get the papers back from him." Tom shook her hand as he showed her out.

Jesse felt a tinge of relief as she stepped out into the growing heat. It was going to be another beautiful day and she wasn't going to waste it—she was going to go and explore the goings-on in Republic.

She walked up one side of Main Street, saying "Hi" to a few of the passersby and turning from most of them. A few women in long dresses would grab their children's hands as they passed her. She caught a few children looking at her like she was a monster.

The streets were quite crowded as she maneuvered down them. The grocery store still had the same name and owner; she grinned as she read the sign. Owned by a group of sisters, it stood against the mountainous backdrop as if it would never change, a true test of time.

The bar had long since been closed down. In fact all five of them had a sign in each window, which read the same: "No drinking allowed by order of the Mayor."

Jesse wondered what power these people really held. Were they witches or wizards? They couldn't turn people into toads. So why on earth had everybody just turned over their way of life to these foreigners?

A new ice cream shop called Screaming Ice Cream appeared to be opening.

"I wish that had been here when I was a kid," Jesse said.

A bunch of all-natural herb shops and bakeries had been added. She walked across the street and stared at a sign that made her giggle. On the window of what used to be a Mexican restaurant a sign was posted in big blinking letters. "All Natural Medicine! Forget The Doctors! Come To Us." She hoped they all caught E. coli and came to them for the cure.

She moved on down the other side of the street and saw more mayoral ordinances posted on signs. She was going to have to ask around as to who was mayor of Republic now.

The drugstore looked dark. She tried the handle and found it to be open. The door buzzed as she stepped into the dark room. The shelves that used to be lined with all sorts of things were almost bare. The shelves behind the counters held very few prescriptions.

"Hello," Jesse yelled. "Anyone here?"

"Yes, be right there." An old woman came from the back room. She had a green dress on and looked to be no less than eighty years old.

"What can I do for you, young lady?" The woman's tone was almost rude. She seemed as cranky of a woman as Jesse had ever met.

"Why does this place look like it's going out of business?" Jesse asked. The drugstore had always been almost like the hallmark of the town. It was one of the wealthiest stores in town when she was growing up.

"It is going out of business. New medicine is coming to town, young lady. No more prescriptions to fill." The woman turned but kept an eye on Jesse as if she thought she might be there to steal from her or something.

Jesse smiled as she turned around. The change of time was evident in all the elders' faces, at least the ones that were still out and about in the community. She felt it was her responsibility to help in any way she could. She had never before been the hero type but now she was changing fast.

"Excuse me, madam." She turned and addressed the woman one last time.

"Yes, what is it young lady?" The woman's tone was agitated now, and Jesse could tell she wished she would just leave and leave her alone but Jesse couldn't do that.

"Could you tell me who's the mayor of this town?" Jesse asked.

"Yes I could, it's Teller Love," the woman answered.

"Teller Love?" Jesse questioned. "What kind of name is that?"

"You're not one of them?" Her tone of voice changed slightly.

"No, I am not one of anyone, I guess. Who is 'them'?" The woman suddenly came to life. A smile crossed her face as she leaned in a little closer to Jesse.

"What's your last name, young lady?"

"Walker. My name is Jessica Walker."

"From Danville?"

"Yes, I am."

"You have the store in Danville. Glad to meet you. I'm Gladys Holmes."

"Nice to meet you, too. Now who are they?"

"All their last names are Love: Hope Love, Jack Love, and Kiss Love and so on and so forth. They all have the same last name and they're everywhere so be careful out there." The old woman smiled as she went back to filling a prescription.

"How many are there in all, do you know?" Jesse moved closer.

The woman turned, her smile broadened. "There are one hundred and fifty-three different families. I have been keeping track for the Anti-Love Organization." Her eyes twinkled and danced. Jesse could tell that she was—how did she put it?—anti-love, one hundred percent and loving it.

"Anti-Love Organization? So how do I get in touch with them and how many of them are there?" Jesse knew that if they were big and many in numbers they might be able to send the cult back to where they came from or at least back to hell if it came to it.

"There are seventy-seven of us, and we have weekly meetings here in the attic. Be here on Wednesday at seven thirty and we will get you informed about the Anti-Love Organization," the woman whispered.

Jesse nodded her reply and left. The streets were still too crowded for Jesse's taste and the people weren't too friendly towards her. The town was still pretty, and from the outside it still looked like a prospecting town.

She slipped into an alley and walked the back way to her truck. She was tired of smiling, trying not to hurt anybody's feelings. She wanted to get home and figure out the rest of this cult mess in the quiet of her own property.

She rounded the bank and made a beeline for her truck. Once behind the wheel, she started her truck and figured she had better get something to eat and head home.

She stopped at the old drive-through, grabbed a hamburger, and headed back to Danville. She had promised Molly she would help her out some today and she didn't want to disappoint her.

She pulled up to the store about one o'clock and noticed Justin's blue pickup out in front.

"Damn it!" she said. He was the last person she wanted to see. "He probably has Karla with him." She didn't need him showing off his girlfriend in front of her right now. After the day at the pond she thought things might be a little better between them. Last night at the bar had been fun, but today she wanted to steer clear of him.

She was tempted to stay in her truck until he left, but she knew that would be childish and she had promised to help Molly. Reluctantly, she stepped from her truck, went inside, and headed straight for the counter.

Molly looked up and saw Jesse coming through the door, her head darting here and there.

"He's out back if you need him." Molly chuckled.

"I don't need him nor do I want to see him," Jesse answered.

"That good, was it?" Molly teased.

"Was what?" Jesse asked as she came behind the counter.

"Nothing, but with you not talking to him and him looking for you, I'm guessing it must have been a good fight." Molly laughed. "Oh, to be young again."

Justin had come into town to look for Jesse and explain Karla being there last night; he had never gotten a chance to explain himself this morning for taking her home last night. He was a little shocked to find her not at the store and worried that something might have happened to her.

He decided to wait around and do some work out back until he heard from her. He watched as she drove up and sat in her truck for a few minutes. He thought she might turn around and head home. He knew he had made her mad taking Karla home, but she had been too drunk to drive herself home.

"Women, they're all the same," he muttered to himself as he tossed a bag of grain into the storage compartment. "One minute they want you, the next minute they want to kill you."

"Oh really? Is that the way we all are, Justin?" Jesse's angry words hit him as he realized he'd said that aloud.

"Jesse, I didn't mean you! I didn't realize you were standing there." Justin tried to backtrack but the rising fury in her face told him to just shut up.

"Go to hell, Justin, and to think I was coming out to apologize for acting so female. Now I don't feel so sorry about it, and I see you for what you are—a jerk!" she screamed as she turned on her heels and marched to her truck.

Justin questioned whether to run after her or not but he figured it would just make things worse. He turned and went back to work. He would talk to her tonight and try to make things better.

Jesse drove straight to Jack's house without realizing it. She drove up the driveway and stopped at the house; it didn't look lived in at all.

The curtains were drawn, and the porch was sagging and didn't look safe. She stepped up carefully on to it and knocked at the door. No answer. She tried the knob and it was locked.

"Jack!" She called. "It's Jesse. Are you here?" No answer. She stepped off the porch and walked around to the back of the house.

When this had been his parents' place it used to be immaculate. His mother had been an excellent gardener and kept the place up well. His father was a carpenter and was always repairing or replacing boards on the old buildings.

She had heard they left the place to Jack and moved to Hawaii on a whim. It seemed a little funny to Jesse at the time and now it looked even stranger. It looked like the yard hadn't been cut in ages and the garden was a mess. The trees and bushes were all overgrown. It appeared like it hadn't been cared for in years.

Maybe Jack was out at the old barn. She decided to look there. As she neared the barn, she heard something moving within.

Jesse hesitated. "Jack, are you in there?" She didn't like the feel of the place at all. Then a thought struck her—maybe he was hurt, or worse, maybe dead.

Creeping into the shadowy barn she stopped and listened for the sound she had heard. A swishing sound was heard from the other end down by the stalls. She crept closer.

It stopped, she stopped. When it started again she crept closer. It was coming from the stall at the end. Was Jack hurt and crawling through the straw?

She ducked down and crept even closer. Suddenly, whatever it was, it stopped. It was a big thing that was making the noise. She waited until it started again, then crept within feet of the stall entrance. The door was ajar with a rope slung across the doorway.

She bit her tongue as she realized that whatever it was, it was directly on the other side of the wall from her. A scream escaped her lips when a large brown muzzle came over the stall side and touched her on the back of the head. Jesse jumped right out of her skin.

"Holy cow! Horse, what are you doing? You scared the pants off me!"

The big bay nuzzled closer to Jesse and she laughed as she scattered kisses along his muzzle.

"You scared me. Jack never said he owned such a sweet beautiful boy like you." Jesse could tell the horse longed for affection by the way he cuddled up next to her.

Jesse ducked under the rope and petted the big bay's neck and shoulder. He turned his head to her and nuzzled closer to her cheek.

"You're so sweet." Jesse's eyes covered the big bay's body. He was in good shape, so someone had to be taking care of him regularly. He had saddle marks on his withers and girth so he had been recently exercised.

Jesse's eyes stung as they settled on the long spur marks on his sides. She ran her hand slowly over them and was shocked to see blood on her fingers. "You poor thing. You're bleeding. If you belong to Jack I'll offer to buy you from him. I promise.

"I have to go find Jack, then maybe I will come back and see you. Next time, I'll bring you some treats. I have a boy at home who you remind me of. You would like Cozy." Jesse said farewell to the big bay and returned to her truck. She figured if she couldn't find Jack to talk to then she would head home and go riding.

* * *

The tall man stepped from behind the barn, a pitchfork in his hand. His face looked like that of a man just winning the lottery.

"Come back soon, honey. Come back real soon. Or maybe I will come see you." His stomach barely moved as he laughed at his own thoughts.

Chapter 11

Back at the Running W, Jesse did not find anybody around and was thankful she didn't have to explain anything before she had the chance to think it through. She wanted to just forget the nasty remarks, forget about Justin, and just ride.

She saddled Cozy and headed to the north pasture. She couldn't keep her mind off of the lady at the pharmacy and her stories of the cult. The "Love" name kept running through her head. She knew she had heard of them before. If she could just remember where, she might be able to do some real investigation on what they were all about.

The Anti-Love Organization fit Jesse in more ways than one. It seemed Anti-Love was her destiny. She figured they could give her the inside scoop on the cult and learn where they lived, what they did, and how they had so much money to buy up everything. All she had to do was wait until Wednesday, if she lived that long without going crazy.

She thought about Justin and how he had said he did not know she was listening and how she found herself running to Jack for a friend. Maybe that meant something in itself.

She thought about Jack's big bay and how he had never said anything about owning a horse or letting the old ranch get so run down. The bay's spur marks unsettled her. Jack had never been a horse lover but she couldn't imagine him spurring a horse to the point of bleeding.

Before she knew it, she had ridden most of the evening until darkness threatened to turn the sky to black. She turned Cozy towards home and let him pick his own pace back, which was a full-out run. She slowed him when she reached the upper gate and made him calm down when she neared the ranch. As she rode around the barn, she was surprised to see so many vehicles parked in front of the house.

Mary and Logan's van and Justin's blue pickup were no surprise. She knew she was going to have to face Justin for dinner and she had prepared for it. However, she had not prepared for Karla or Jack to be there.

Where was Jack when she needed him, and why the hell was Karla there? She secretly wished she could tell the slut to saddle up and ride away with Justin in tow.

Slipping from the saddle, she led Cozy into the barn. She pulled the saddle from his back and gave him a scoop of grain to entertain him as she brushed him from head to tail.

She didn't want to go inside and face Karla or Jack right now. Most of all, however, she really didn't want to see Justin or hear him make Karla laugh or watch as she took his arm and smiled at him. The thought of those two together made her want to puke.

"May I sleep with you tonight, Cozy?" He turned and gave her a nuzzle as if to say, only if you keep brushing me. Jesse laughed and put the brush away.

"I guess I had better go face them. Tomorrow Marnie will be here and then we can ignore them all weekend. Oh, how fun it will be. You like Marnie, don't you boy?" she asked as she scratched his belly with her hand. He turned his nose up and leaned into her.

"I had better go or soon they'll send out the police after me. Not that they could find shit if they put their hands in it, but nonetheless, I had better go. See you later. I love you."

Jesse shut Cozy's stall and turned off the lights, then ambled towards the house, not at all eager to get inside. She hesitated at the steps and looked through the large window. She could see everybody already sitting at the table, their plates cleaned of the last of their dessert crumbs.

She silently praised Mary for being so on time with dinner. Now all she had to do was slip in, grab a plate, and head to her bedroom. She opened the door and stepped into the lion's den.

"Hey, there you are! We almost gave up and called the police to come find you," Mary scolded.

"Sorry, I lost track of time."

"You could have gotten a lot of people hurt because you lost track of time. You know it's dangerous and yet you go off riding without telling anybody where you were," Justin barked.

He had been so afraid she might have been hurt or killed he had been pacing the floor ever since Mary told him she wasn't here. He hadn't meant to scold her as soon as she walked in, but relief flooded him when he saw her. He couldn't tell by the look on her face if he had hurt her feelings or pissed her off. He wished he could, but her face told him nothing.

Logan could tell you what was about to hit the fan. He had been just as relieved as Justin was when he saw Jesse walk through the front door, but he wasn't sure scolding a grown woman for riding on her own land was the way to handle it.

"Jesse, everybody was just worried, we're all glad to see you're okay. Are you hungry?" Logan tried to soothe the tension a little.

Jesse knew he was trying to change the subject and it was working because the minute she had opened the door she smelled steak and corn. She didn't want to let Justin off for being an ass, but she would confront him later. One thing Hank had taught her was to never belittle a man in front of anyone.

"Starving, Logan. I'm sorry for worrying you and Mary."

She ignored Justin and ignored him in her apology. The fact that he could bring that slut around to her house after last night pissed her off.

"I'll make you a plate," Mary added as she headed to the kitchen and prepared a plate full of corn, a steak, and mashed potatoes topped off with a hearty homemade biscuit and gravy. It didn't take Jesse long to gobble it up, say her thanks, and try to retreat to her room alone.

"I'm tired. If you will excuse me."

She stood and was bid adieu by a round of goodnights. She watched as Justin eyed her and could tell he wanted to talk to her but he had enough to keep his hands full for the night. Jack watched her the same way but he was a bit bolder; he stood and came to meet her.

"May I walk you up? I would like to talk to you about a few things."

Jesse looked over at Justin, who she could tell didn't like the idea of Jack in her room at all.

"Yes, I think it will be all right," Jesse responded, and accepted Jack's arm as he led her down the hallway and toward the stairs. She did it mostly to annoy Justin, but partially because she was so curious about the state of the old ranch.

"What can I do for you, Jack?"

"I wanted to know why you left me last night." Jack had been pissed he hadn't been able to put his plan into action.

"I was tired and you looked like you were having fun with Karla." Jesse knew she was going to have to explain leaving him some day but she would have rather not done it tonight. That was going to have to be a good enough excuse for now.

She knew she had no feelings for Jack. It was just the fact that Justin hated him so much that she kept telling herself to let him hang around. She didn't want to hurt his feelings, so she would allow him to hang around awhile longer.

"Can we talk about this another day? I'm really tired."

Jack wanted to press the issue but he really wanted to get her closer to her room and spend a while there just to make that busybody Justin jealous. But he didn't want to push her too much or she might not ever want to see him again.

"Very well, get your sleep. We can talk sometime soon, maybe for lunch?"

"Yes, that sounds great. Goodnight, Jack."

"Goodnight, sweet Jess." He brushed a light kiss across her cheek that made her skin crawl. He turned and headed back down the hallway.

"Jack," Jesse called.

"Yes. What is it?"

"I didn't know you owned a horse."

"I don't."

"But when I went to see you today there was a big bay in your barn." Jesse was a bit confused.

"If he was then he was lost, or somebody is staying at my old place without my approval. I don't have a horse and I haven't been back to the old homestead for about two years. A caretaker looks after it for me."

"He isn't doing a very good job of it, then. The place is a mess."

"I'll have to go have a look at it."

"Do that. And if you're paying the guy anything I would fire him, because he isn't worth a dollar."

Jack hated the house and everything that was on that place. It reminded him of his parents and that was a bad thing. He had fought for them all he could to keep them out of a nursing home.

His brother Gus had insisted they be sent to a home, so they spread the word around the community that they were moving to Hawaii.

Gus had been in the Marines most of Jack's childhood. He had never even seen him until he was twelve. Gus called and wrote many times, but he hated Danville and swore he would never come back home. He had given his half of the estate to Jack for just that reason.

"Well where do you live now?"

"Above my gym. I own the training center in Republic."

"That explains a lot, but you had better go check on that horse and make sure he's okay. He has some nasty spur marks on him. If you need any help, call me. Goodnight, Jack."

"I'll run over tonight and check on the place. I'll call you if I need anything. Goodnight again, Jess." With that, he opened the door and left.

Jesse quickly made it to her room and changed into a shirt and shorts.

"Let's see who the lucky woman is tonight," she said as she picked up her book. Flipping to page thirty, she almost screamed in horror as she read the woman's name.

"Karla? That figures." She laughed to herself despite the lack of humor in the situation. She forced herself to read about the half-hearted guy and Karla the curvaceous redhead from Boston who didn't know how ripe she looked.

Jesse was definitely going to ask Marnie for that dictionary. She wondered how a woman could look "ripe." As she looked at the mirror on top of the dresser what she saw looked tanned and tired, not ripe at all.

She finished reading about the "throes of passion" featuring Karla and the half-hearted guy and wished she had read a different chapter tonight instead of that one. It just made her madder thinking of the other Karla downstairs wanting to jump into the throes of passion with Justin.

"I hate that name... Karla. Yuck."

Hate and rage soon drove Jesse to sleep. She dreamed of dead cows and being entangled in rope and drowning in kisses. She woke around two o'clock in a cold sweat and opened the window to get a cool breeze and saw a light moving in the barn.

"Justin, what are you doing now?" she thought.

She rushed out of the house to see what was happening in the new barn. Maybe a mare was foaling or somebody was sick. She turned the corner and realized the light was coming from Cozy's stall. She heard two voices that she didn't know. Both sounded male. One was somewhat familiar but she could not put a name to it.

"Are you sure this is the one?" she heard one man say in a thick, gruff voice.

"Yes, I'm sure I've seen him before," the other replied. His voice was more nasal in tone.

"Well, it shouldn't be long now," the first man said.

"Hurry before someone wakes up," the second man said. "Can't we go any faster?"

"No, it takes time," the first one said in an angry tone.

"Hey, what's going on?" she yelled.

The flashlight went off and the voices stopped. The whole barn was in total darkness.

"I'm going to call the police," she yelled again. "Get out of here, now!" She turned around and ran to the light switch, and instantly the whole barn was flooded with light. She picked up a pitchfork and ran to Cozy's stall but nobody was there. She dropped the pitchfork and screamed in horror.

Chapter 12

Cozy lay on the floor with blood pouring into a container at the base of his throat, but he wasn't dead. She pulled off her shirt and stuffed it into the wound.

"Don't worry boy, you'll be okay, I promise," she sobbed.

She ran to the house and phoned the vet, waking him out of a deep sleep. After telling him the situation, he told her he was on his way and to keep pressure on the wound. She phoned Justin and left a message on his answering machine. Over the intercom she screamed for Logan to come to the barn and to hurry.

She knew she had to keep her head straight and stop crying or she was going to be of no use to Cozy. Her best friend in the whole world was lying in a stall bleeding to death, and the two guys responsible were getting away.

She ran back out to Cozy, sunk down next to him in the straw and stroked his neck with one hand as she kept pressure on the wound with the other.

"Please don't die, old man. We've been through a lot together. Please don't die," she begged of him.

The sirens were coming up the road and Jesse figured the vet must have called the sheriff. She watched in horror as Cozy's eyes closed for the last time. His final breath was swift. His chest stopped moving. Jesse collapsed on his neck and sobbed.

"No! Cozy, don't do it, don't die! Help is on the way. Wake up!" She sobbed uncontrollably on his shoulder.

Justin was sound asleep when Jesse's quaking voice woke him up. "Please come to the new barn, I need you," she said. Justin was surprised to see the vet and the sheriff standing in the breezeway as he stepped inside.

"What's wrong?" he asked. "Where's Jesse? What happened?" No one answered. They just looked towards Cozy's stall.

"Jess! Where are you?"

The vet pointed to Cozy's stall. Justin ran the short distance and turned to find Jesse sobbing uncontrollably with her face down in her beloved gelding's neck, her hands covered in blood. She wore just a bra and no shirt. He could see it was stuffed into a gaping wound at the gelding's throat. Blood flowed over a container at the gelding's neck and stained the boards and straw.

Justin knelt down and touched Jesse's shoulder, and it was cold. He took off his jacket and placed it over her shoulders.

"Jesse, I'm sorry, I will find the bastard responsible for this and make them pay, I promise."

Jesse looked up at him with bloodshot eyes. She believed him and she knew he would help. But right now that did not help the burning in her throat or eyes.

"I saw a flashlight on in here. I thought it was you. I yelled at them but they vanished before I could reach the light switch. Why him, Justin, why Cozy?" She collapsed back down upon her beloved friend's corpse.

"I can't answer that. I wish I could."

"He has never hurt anyone. Why him?"

Justin looked at the sheriff.

"Good question. Why Cozy out of all the horses in this barn? He wasn't the closest one to a door, if anything he was the farthest away from one."

The sheriff was a big man, and fat rolled from his chin to his chest. He didn't look like a particularly good person and he didn't seem to be a good sheriff either. He hemmed and hawed about who, what, and why, then he took a few names and made a few comments and left.

The vet took some blood samples and expressed his sympathy to Jesse. He looked over the rest of the horses to make sure no others were hurt.

"I'll get these samples to the lab and I should know more about how this happened. We'll catch them, Jesse, you can count on it." The vet turned and headed for a long night's work in his lab.

Justin sat next to Jess for about an hour. His teeth started to chatter and he knew Jesse had to be cold as well.

"Jesse, we need to go to the house and warm up," Justin stammered through chattering teeth.

"I'm staying right here," Jesse insisted.

"Jesse, if you don't come inside you're going to freeze. If I promise to help you make a box and bury Cozy tomorrow morning will you please come inside with me?"

Jesse was momentarily caught off guard.

"You would help me do that?" Most people would just drag him out, leave him in some ravine somewhere, and let the buzzards eat him. She had planned on burying him but hadn't realized the thought would even cross Justin's mind.

"If something happened to Badger, I would make sure he got buried."

"Really?" Jesse asked.

"I wouldn't expect anything less from you."

"Thank you."

"I promise I will help you do that tomorrow or when you wake up, no matter what. Can we please go to the house? I'm freezing."

Jesse looked up to find poor Justin in just a T-shirt and shaking horribly. She had almost forgotten that he had placed his jacket around her shoulders until she looked down and realized she had on only a bra beneath.

"Yes, let's go get you warm."

Jesse stroked Cozy's neck one last time, kissed him on the shoulder, and stood.

"He was a great horse."

Justin felt the pain in Jesse's voice. "I know he was, and he will be missed by many."

Justin wrapped an arm around her waist and they walked back to the house together. Once inside, Jesse went to heating some water for coffee and turning up the heat for Justin. He shivered uncontrollably, as did she, but she shook from the new stream of tears that rolled down her cheeks. Justin crossed to her and wrapped her in his arms, resting his cheek against her head. He chattered on about sweet nothings that made Jesse weak at the knees.

"Why did you bring Karla here to flaunt in front of me?" Jesse asked against his chest.

Justin stepped back and stared down at her as Jesse turned to face him.

"The same reason you invited Jack out to dance the other night and the same reason he came out last night. I wanted to forget about that day at the pond. I needed to put distance between you and me somehow."

"I hoped Jack would help me forget about you."

"Did it work?"

"I thought it did, but here I am, back in your arms again. Jack is an old love that died out long ago, that's all."

"I've never cared for Karla at all."

"Then why did you sleep with her that night when we came home from dancing?" Jesse accused.

Jesse remembered only one rig leaving that night. She knew he had taken her to his house and then she shivered as she thought of what he probably did to her.

"I never slept with her. She wanted me to, begged me to take her to my house, but I took her home. She was way too drunk and I knew she shouldn't be driving. Is that why you've been so mad at me?"

"That and the remark at the store." Jesse was still pissed off at that little remark.

"I was mad and frustrated at the whole situation, please forgive me for that. I like having you for a friend and I don't want you mad at me over anything."

"You're forgiven, and thank you for being here tonight with me." Jesse wasn't sure she would have made it back to the house tonight had it not been for Justin reminding her she was cold.

"I'm here for whatever you need, as long as you promise me something."

"What?" Jesse questioned.

"That you will forget about Jack for a while. I don't like him and I wonder if he is behind some of these things that are happening."

"Jack! No, not him, I mean it couldn't be. Why would he be so danged sweet one moment and kill my cows much less my horse the next?"

"Sweet? I have never known Jack and sweet to be in the same sentence."

"Are you jealous, Justin?"

"Not of Jack. I'm twice the man he'll ever dream of being."

"Then who are you jealous of?"

"No one. But I wish you would take my advice and forget him, at least for a couple days."

"You know I think I might be able to do that for a few days." Jesse tried to smile through her tear-stained face.

"Good. Now that he is out of your head, I can keep your mind on the important things in life."

"Like what?"

"Me," Justin said as he lowered his face to hers and brushed a light kiss across her lips. She leaned into him and deepened the kiss. He slipped his tongue through her parted lips.

"Oh God, help me," Jesse murmured.

"You're right, we need to stop." Justin moaned as he pulled away and looked down at her.

"Do you care for me?" Jesse asked.

"More than I should, but I can't love you, Jess, not ever. I'm no good."

"But you said you were twice the man Jack dreamed he was and he thinks he is good enough for me."

"He's wrong. He isn't even worth the lint in your pockets, and neither am I."

"I wish I could have seen you prior to whatever woman killed your heart."

"I wish I had known you before Hank."

"I wish Hank was just a dream."

"If I ever come across him I'll punch him in the nose for you," Justin said.

"I want to forget about the past. I just want you right now," Jesse said.

"I am just a one-night man with no commitment the next morning and I could never do that kind of thing to you." Justin knew he was telling her too much, but he wanted her to know why he couldn't love her like she needed to be loved.

"Why are you no good? Please tell me," Jesse whispered into his neck as she pulled him a little closer.

"No, Jesse. Just know that in the last few days I have fallen in love with you as much as I could ever love a decent woman." Justin loosened his embrace.

Jesse turned and welcomed the new batch of tears to her eyes. She cried for Cozy, she cried for Justin's half a heart, and for her damned cowgirl pride that wouldn't allow her to be a one-night stand.

She wanted Justin and needed Justin but her pride just wouldn't allow her to be used again for pleasure without a return of some kind of affection and love.

She poured water into two cups and placed an instant coffee bag in each. She handed one to Justin and took one herself and they sat in silence staring at each other across the table.

Jesse was about to break the silence when Logan burst through the door.

"What happened? I was sound asleep when I heard the intercom. It took me a while to wake up and get outside."

"They killed Cozy." A new burst of tears ran down her cheeks as she told Logan the story. When she finished, he hugged her briefly and sat down to think.

"You say you heard two guys. Right, Jesse?" Logan questioned. "And one you said sounded familiar."

"Would you recognize the voice if you heard it again?" Justin asked.

"Yes, I think so. Why, what are you two thinking?"

"Tomorrow we'll bury Cozy in the morning and then spend the whole day in town listening," Justin said.

"Marnie is supposed to be here tomorrow."

"Who's Marnie?" Justin asked.

"She's my best friend. Tomorrow she's coming up to bring me my other three broodmares."

"Then we'll all go to lunch and walk around afterwards."

"Who's 'we,' Justin?" Jesse asked.

"You, Marnie, and me, we'll go to lunch at the café and stop by the Old Crow and just listen. Republic or wherever we have to go but we will catch them, you can count on that."

"That's right, Jessica. We'll catch the bastards who killed Cozy and make them pay," Logan said as his heart ached for the little girl he knew and loved as if she was his own daughter.

"To get some justice, we'll hang them from the highest tree on this place if we have to," Justin stated. Jesse loved the way he was so much on her side. He was caring and perfect in every aspect when he was like this.

"Okay, Justin, tomorrow we'll go out and listen. Just you and Marnie and me."

"Well, if you two are okay, I'm going to head for the bunkhouse for a few more hours of sleep," Logan stated as he headed for the door. "See you two in the morning. Jess, I am sorry for your loss, and if there is anything we can do let us know. He will be missed around here."

"Thanks, Logan. Goodnight." With that, he stepped out into the cold night air and headed for the bunkhouse.

"I guess I should be going, too. Are you sure you're going to be okay?" Justin stood next to the sink emptying the rest of his cup into it. Jesse joined him and placed a hand on his shoulder.

"No, I'm not sure. Would you mind staying and talking for a while longer? I don't want to be alone," Jesse said.

"Not at all. Shall we watch a movie? I think something funny would be a good change to everything that has happened already today."

"Okay, something funny it is then. I'll make some popcorn."

"I'll get a couple of beers."

"Beer?" Jesse questioned. "It's two o'clock in the morning. You sure you want to break open the beer?"

"I think it would mellow us out, don't you? But I don't think popcorn goes with beer."

Jesse looked at him with a slight smile on her face. He was an unusual man. Sometimes he was as hard as polished steel, other times he was as sweet and fun as a baby.

"I think I saw some red wine in the pantry, do you think that would go better?" Jesse asked with a smile.

"Popcorn and red wine? Why, I'm sure that is the food of gods. I'll go see if I can find the wine in the pantry."

Jesse and Justin each departed on their own quest.

It didn't take long to find the bottle of red wine and a couple glasses. Justin was flipping through the channels when Jesse joined him on the couch with a bowl of popcorn.

"Here, want some popcorn?" Jesse asked as she offered him the bowl.

"Find anything good to watch on TV?"

"No. A couple of romantic comedies, but none that are just funny without all that mumbo-jumbo love stuff."

Jesse couldn't help but smile at him all stretched out on the sofa next to her looking so damn sexy in his Wranglers and white T-shirt. He talked so tough with his no-love policy even though Jesse knew he was as willing as she had been a couple of days ago at the pond. The kiss in the kitchen had been telling of his feelings, if she could just get him to forget about his past love. She knew he was hurt pretty bad by it but life was going to go on.

She watched his chest rise and fall with each breath he took, its chiseled features evident beneath the thin white cotton shirt.

The day's growth of stubble that covered his face gave him a tough, handsome look. The disarrangement of his hair told of the fact that he had been in bed when Jesse called.

"Justin?"

"What is it, Jess?" he asked as he looked down at her nestled next to him on the couch.

"Thank you."

"For what?"

"For coming over to help me tonight and for staying around." Jesse hadn't remembered if she had thanked him or not for being the shoulder that she had cried on. She figured the floor or couch was her only other bet if he hadn't been there, but he was much softer and warmer.

"I want them dead for what they did." Jesse couldn't help letting a few tears fall down her cheek at the thought of her dear Cozy being dead.

Justin saw the new stream of tears fall down her face and couldn't help but reach out and wipe them away with the palm of his hand. Her skin was so soft and warm against his weathered hands.

"Please don't cry." Justin couldn't stand to see one more tear fall from her eyes. He knew that if the day came when he came face to face with the bastard that killed her gelding he was going to see that he hurt before he called the police to come get his tattered carcass.

Justin leaned in and brushed his lips across hers very briefly and gently. The meaning behind it was merely a tear stopper, nothing more.

That was all he meant to do. But her lips were so soft and inviting against his that he had to kiss her again, this time not so briefly or so gently. His mouth covered hers, searching, seeking, wanting more. His blood heated as she melted against him.

She was so inviting as she threw her arms around Justin's neck and deepened the kiss even more.

Her body was on fire as Justin ran his hands down her side and beneath her shirt. Jesse longed for him to whisper that he wanted her forever and that she was safe with him, but she knew it would never happen. He had already said he was only a one night stand man, no commitments.

She knew she couldn't resist his kisses or the urge of his body against hers and she wanted him more than anything else right then. With a quick movement she was straddling Justin's lap, and she could feel his engorged manhood against her thigh.

Justin urged her lips apart and when Jesse complied, he slipped his warm, sleek tongue inside her mouth. She quivered and responded by deepening the kiss even more and throwing her arms around his neck.

Jesse knew that if she was going to stop she had to do it now or her willpower might not let her do it later. She stopped kissing him and pulled away, and sat still across his lap, staring at him.

Justin looked up into her face. He could see mixed emotions stirring there and knew she was doing the best thing by stopping it from going any farther; he wasn't the man she needed.

"I'm sorry, Jesse, I hadn't planned on that happening again."

She shocked him when she looked straight into his eyes and replied so brazenly, "I did."

"You what?"

"I wanted that to happen, Justin, and more. I know you said you only wanted a one night stand, so…"

"So what, Jess? I don't want to treat you like that, you deserve better. Much better than me, and I refuse to commit, you know that."

"You're what I want. And if one night is all I can have of you, I'll take it, no commitment needed." Jesse had thought about it and she wanted to feel him against her all night, even if in the morning he was gone. She wanted to hold him tonight.

"Jesse, it's just a one night stand I want, with no commitment. In the morning I am going to saddle up and ride away."

"Wow, a real cowboy. Justin, I don't care. I don't want any commitment either. Yes, some day I would like to find a man to be with forever, have babies and grow old with, but right now I just want someone to hold once in a while. One night, I don't think so, but maybe one night at a time with no commitment."

Justin pulled her down to him and kissed her hard on the lips. "One night at a time. We can do that, if that's what you're sure you want."

"I'm sure, but I need a shower before I even go the first night." Jesse looked at her hands and shorts, which still had traces of Cozy's blood on them. A gruesome reminder of what she had waiting for her in the morning. She looked back up at Justin, her eyes again misting over with unshed tears.

Justin stood up, pulled Jesse up into his arms, and carried her up the stairs. Jesse rested her head against his shoulder, thankful for the sturdiness of his shoulder to cry on.

"What do you know, I need one too."

He set her on the bed and left the room without a word to turn on the shower. After a few moments, he returned.

Chapter 13

Justin said, "If you don't mind, I'm going to go take a look through the barn again and make sure everything is okay. I've started the shower for you. I'll take one when I come back."

He had a strange feeling that something wasn't right and just had to go see for himself. He knew that Jesse offered something he wanted badly, but he just had to set his mind at ease first.

"Okay. Do you want me to go with you?"

"No, you've seen enough tonight. Take your shower, warm up, and I'll come find you after I take mine."

"All right, if that's what you want."

Jesse wasn't sure if this was just his way of running out on her or if he truly was worried about something. But one way or the other she had to let him go. She would just have to wait and see if he came back.

"Hey, I'll be right back, I promise. I just have to put my mind at ease. I want to check on Boe and Catchy again and I need to check on the fawn. I forgot to check him when we were in the barn."

"Okay, be careful."

"I will."

Justin lowered his head and brushed a light kiss across her lips. Shivers raced down Jesse's spine, but as soon as the kiss had begun, it ended. When she opened her eyes, he was already gone.

"Oh my god, Marnie's books are right."

Out in the barn Justin had left the lights on and the radio playing. He was relieved a little to hear George Straight singing, "Where the sidewalk ends."

He really had wanted to get the tractor and load Cozy so that Jess didn't have to see it happen in the morning. He walked down the aisle looking into every stall. The stallions were nervous, probably from the smell of blood that still hung heavy in the air.

The fawn was sound asleep in the hay. Maggie and her baby were up and both eating. Justin talked to her awhile before moving on down the aisle. He stopped at Cozy's stall and was surprised to find it open. He was sure he had closed it when they left.

He knew something was off when a set of bloody footprints and a strange blood trail grabbed his attention. Somebody had been here after he left. He looked in at Cozy and almost threw up. Someone had come back and decapitated him.

He ran to the house and phoned the police again. After relaying his message and the details of what he saw, the deputy said he would be right out and not to touch anything.

Justin didn't want to tell Jess but he knew he was going to have to. He slowly climbed the stairs and peeked into her bedroom. She wasn't there, and he realized she was most likely still in the shower.

"Jess!" he said as he entered the bathroom.

"Yes?" she said from inside the shower. "Still need a shower? Come on in."

"Jess, something happened and I need to tell you about it before the police get here."

"Don't tell me it's Boe this time." Her voice quaked as she spoke. Justin was glad he didn't have to tell her anything else had been murdered.

"No, nothing else has been killed, it's just that while we were in the house they came back to Cozy's stall."

"What did they do to him?" She was tearing up fast; he could tell by her voice.

"They decapitated him. The police are on their way." He waited for a reply but the shower stall was quiet. "Jess, I'm sorry."

"I'm going to kill them, every single one of them. Not even the worms will find their bodies." Jesse was pissed more than anything. They couldn't just leave Cozy alone. Now they had to come back and cut off his head. She was going to get even with them any way she could.

"I'm going to help you, Jess."

"Good. Once we figure out who killed him I am going to make them wish they hadn't messed with me."

"Here's a towel. Get dressed—we're going to follow a blood trail." Justin handed a towel over the side of the shower to Jesse. "I'll meet you downstairs."

"I'll be down in a few minutes. Hey Justin, tomorrow I want to go talk to Bill. I stopped in the other day but something wasn't right. He said he had company and he pretended he didn't know me."

"Okay, that won't be too hard. With him living in town, maybe he'll know something." Justin turned and headed to the kitchen to wait for the police and Jesse. He didn't like the idea of having Jesse's friend Marnie added to the mix as well. He would prefer to keep her well away from trouble.

It didn't take long for Jesse to get dressed and join Justin downstairs. She had a rifle slung over one shoulder and a bullet belt around her narrow hips. If it hadn't been such a tragic incident that made her don the gunfighter attire, he would have laughed at how sexy she looked in her getup.

"I grabbed a couple flashlights. Here's one for you." She handed him a flashlight and smiled at the gleam in his eyes. She knew he wanted to say something about her attire but she knew he wouldn't unless asked.

"Say it, Justin, get it off your chest now."

"What are you talking about?"

"I know you want to say something about my getup, so say it now and get it over with."

He covered the distance between them in a matter of a stride. One arm grabbed her by the waist and the other her neck and he pulled her to him and kissed her in a savage need for lust. Her knees went weak, and she realized he was all that was holding her up. After a few bold thrusts of his tongue, he released her.

"You look damn sexy dressed like Annie Oakley."

He smiled down at her and she wrapped her arms around his neck and turned her face into his shoulder. He held on to her until he heard the sirens approaching.

"Guess we had better get going."

"Yeah. Are you going to tell the deputy we're tracking the blood trail this morning?"

"I was hoping he would come with us."

"Good idea."

Once they said their hellos to the deputy, Justin showed him Cozy while Jesse stayed back. She had no urge or desire to see him decapitated.

"Where's the head?" the deputy asked. "I thought it was just cut off, not stolen."

Jesse had thought the same thing. She cringed at the idea of burying Cozy without his head.

"I have no idea. We're going to follow the blood trail tonight and hopefully see if we can find it or the guys who did this."

"I think I should come along."

"We would be glad to have you."

Justin laid the sheet back over Cozy and turned to look at Jesse, who had grown paler. He could tell she wasn't as tough as she looked when it came to her lifelong friend being killed.

"Jess, if you want, you can go back to the house and wait. I'll call you if we find anything."

"No, I want to come. I don't want to be alone."

"Okay, but tell me at any time if you would like to come back to the house."

"Okay." She smiled a weak smile at him to let him know that she was all right. He returned her smile with a much better one. His blue eyes twinkled as he gazed at her.

The deputy took a few more photos, called in his location, and told his base he was going to follow the blood trail. After receiving the authority to do so, all three started out. The trail was easy to follow; they must have dragged Cozy's head instead of packing it.

They followed it past the back fields and under the border fence. Every now and then the deputy would shut off his light and make everyone stop so he could listen. They knew they couldn't be more than an hour or two behind them, and with any luck they would catch them along the way.

The trail was leading towards Justin's place. Everybody realized it, but nobody said anything until his house lights were visible ahead of them.

"Did you leave your lights on, Justin?"

"Yes, those are my kitchen and my porch lights. I always leave those two on."

"Justin?" Jesse whispered. "Why would someone drag his head to your place?"

"I don't know, but I think we're going to find out soon."

As they neared the house Justin was alarmed at the fact that his dog, Jinks, didn't come running out to bark at them.

"Stop, deputy. My dog isn't barking. That means one of two things: he hasn't heard us, or he's dead."

"I hope it's the first," Jesse answered.

"Me too."

"Let's creep around the perimeter of the house first and then we'll move in," said the deputy.

The perimeter showed no movement and so they moved in towards the back door. The deputy's gun was drawn and Jess had her hand on her own.

At the back door, they stopped again to listen but all they heard was a bird somewhere in the morning darkness singing for the break of day. Jesse had to agree she wished the daylight would come as well.

The deputy tried the doorknob and found it was open.

"I never lock the back door," Justin whispered.

They stepped inside and listened again. The deputy switched the light on and they all stood waiting for something horrible to be found.

The living room looked normal. Jesse found it a lot tidier than she would have thought. A large leather sofa faced away from them towards a large-screen television covering the wall. A leather chair sat facing the same direction. A large cougar hide covered another wall, and deer heads with enormous antlers were scattered here and there. The place was nicely decorated and showed of some money going into it.

The dining room and kitchen were as nice as the living room. Two guns crisscrossed over the dinette set. In the kitchen, pots and pans filled the racks and nice dinnerware was visible through clear glass cupboard doors.

A big fridge stood between the dishwasher and sink. Jesse smiled; Justin had great taste. She looked over at Justin, whose eyes were focused at the fridge along with the deputy's. She looked back and saw what they were focused on.

At the bottom of the fridge, a small pool of blood was evident. The deputy stepped over and opened the fridge, and as he did he turned and vomited in the sink.

"Justin, call for backup, now!" he said as he vomited again.

Chapter 14

The deputy had refused to let them look in the fridge but assured them the search for Cozy's head and Jinks were over. Jesse and Justin sat on the sofa waiting for the investigation to be over.

"Justin, Jesse, could we talk to you for a few moments?" the sheriff asked after the fridge had been removed from the kitchen.

"Yes, of course," Justin replied.

Jesse nodded and waited for the questions to begin. She knew one of them was going to be, "Where was Justin during all of this?"

"Justin, why did you go out to the barn again this morning?"

"I was over at Jesse's and I just felt like I had to go take another look at the stallions."

"How long were you outside before you went back in and told Jess about Cozy?"

"Maybe about an hour."

"It took you an hour to find Cozy?"

"No, I checked the stallions and grabbed a sheet to put over Cozy. We found a fawn whose mother died so I checked on him and a mare who had just had a foal. I talked to her awhile. The stallions were nervous so I calmed them down a bit, then I went to Cozy's stall and found him that way. That's when I called the police and told Jesse."

"Is there anyone you two might have made mad in the past few weeks?"

"Officer, I have only been here for almost four days, and I have met no one new. Don't you think maybe it was the cult?"

"I don't know, Jesse. However, I want you two to be very careful who you talk to and where you go in the next few weeks. Along with the head and a mutilated dog was a note."

"A note?" Jesse asked.

"What did it say, Sheriff?"

"'Next time the bullet won't miss,' something to that effect. Someone wants you two dead. I don't know who, but lock your barns and your doors, and if you two are romantically involved as the note also implies, you might want to stick together. You're going to be safer together."

"What else did the letter say, Sheriff?" Justin could tell there was more he didn't want to say.

"I will read it to you if you really want to hear it. I guess you both should know what's going on."

He took out a zip-lock bag from his briefcase. Inside was a letter covered in blood.

To the bastard on the gray horse,

Next time you leave your little woman unattended she won't be there to run down the hill when you call. And the next time you decide to hump her, the bullet won't miss.

Hope you like what I left for dinner, maybe you two can eat it with some popcorn and red wine. Your poor little doggie was a little tough so I cut him up for you. I hear horse is delicious.

"He must have been watching us from the window."

"Why do you think that, Jesse?" the sheriff asked.

"Because we ate popcorn and red wine as we sat down to watch a movie." The thought of someone watching them from the window made Jesse nauseous.

"Did he sign the letter?" Justin asked.

"He signed the letter 'Love,' with no name."

"He left a name," Jesse answered.

"What? We never saw one."

"Love, that's his name."

"Love is his name?"

"Yes, his last name anyway. I talked to this lady who owns the drugstore in Republic—she said that the last name of everybody in the cult is 'Love.' She even said that your mayor's name was Teller Love. She said there was Hope Love, Faith Love, Jack Love, and Kiss Love, too. She said all of them had the last name of Love."

Justin looked at her inquisitively. "When did you talk to her, Jess?"

"Yesterday, just after I went to the lawyer's office and filed for a divorce."

"Where does your husband live?" the sheriff asked.

"Caldwell, but he doesn't know I'm up here. He doesn't even know I still own the ranch."

"Well, I don't have any more questions for you two. Just stick close to home and don't wander into town very often, just in case. We won't be done fingerprinting here for a while, so if you want I could drive you back over to the Running W."

"That would be great," Justin said.

They climbed into the back seat of the patrol car. Jesse laid her head against Justin's chest.

"What time is it, Justin?" Jesse knew it had to be close to four in the morning. She was so tired and ready to sleep all day if allowed.

"Four-thirty. Tired?" He wrapped an arm around her shoulders and pulled her closer. They thanked the sheriff for the ride and found their way upstairs to Jesse's bedroom.

Jesse pulled her boots off and threw her jacket on the floor. She crawled into bed and collapsed into the mattress.

Justin pulled off his boots and crawled in next to her.

"Goodnight, Justin."

"Good morning, Jesse. Remember, it's four-thirty."

She rolled over and sleep claimed her. Justin listened to her breathing even out until sleep drifted over him as well. The morning sun and the roosters crowing didn't stir the sleeping couple until well into the afternoon.

Jesse rolled over and was momentarily shocked to find Justin still sleeping next to her. She quietly got out of bed and changed clothes while he slept. She watched him for a few moments before she crept from the bedroom and headed to the barn to check on Boe. Somehow, she had expected to be the one waking up to an empty bed.

The afternoon air was crisp and refreshing, and when she reached the barn she was surprised to see Logan had the tractor in the aisle. She knew what he was doing and was glad for his help. When she neared Cozy's stall she realized he was already gone and so was all the bloody straw. She could tell Logan had washed down the floor with some disinfectant.

"Good morning, Jessica," Logan said as he rounded the stall door pushing a wheelbarrow full of shavings.

"Where's Cozy?" Jesse asked, suddenly worried that maybe he was just laying somewhere.

"I dug a hole with the backhoe this morning and built a box for him. You'll be happy to know he is all there in the box. The sheriff stopped by this morning and placed everything in the box. I didn't want to bother you so I placed him in the hole. I haven't covered it yet in case you wanted to add something."

"Thank you, I do want to add something, his bridle. I would like it placed in the box with him. No other horse will ever wear it."

"If you get it for me, I will see it gets done."

"Thank you. I'll go get it."

"Oh, Jessica. The sheriff is worried about you. I heard the whole story and I want you to be careful."

"I will."

Jesse strode out of the barn and to the house. She crept upstairs to see if Justin had woken up yet. She crept in the bedroom and stood watching him sleep. The steady rise and fall of his chest made her want to sit down and watch him.

She did just that until she heard the rattle of a rig coming down the driveway. She knew that could only be one person. She jumped up and ran downstairs, taking a few of the steps two at a time. She ran from the house and was happy to see Marnie driving up with the horse trailer rattling along behind.

When the truck pulled to a halt Marnie dove from the door and jumped into Jesse's arms.

"Jess! I missed you and I have great news!"

Marnie had planned on telling Jess over dinner that she was going to live with her but she was so excited she couldn't wait.

"What's the great news, Marnie?" Jesse asked as she hugged her friend. She figured she would wait awhile before she told Marnie about Cozy. Marnie had always loved Cozy about as much as she had.

"I quit my job."

"You did? I'm so proud of you." Jesse knew that Marnie had hated working for the bank; they had always taken advantage of her skills.

"And, I sold my house." Marnie jumped up and down and Jesse could tell she was excited.

"You did what?"

"I sold my house."

"I heard you. I just can't believe it, you loved that house."

"I know. But do you want to know what I'm going to do now?"

"Yes I do." Jesse couldn't believe it. Marnie had never been the type of person to do anything on a whim, especially just sell everything and pack up her belongings. She had always seemed so happy with her life in Caldwell.

"I am going to move in with you. I'll cook and clean and do whatever it is you need me to do. I will help you with your finances on the store and I'll work there, too."

"Oh my gosh, you're going to stay here with me, forever?"

Jesse was so happy. She loved Marnie and could use her help and friendship.

"Is this a forever move-in or just until you decide to move on, Marnie?"

"Forever, Jess, or until I'm just a third wheel." Marnie was looking at the handsome man who had stepped out onto the porch where Jess had come from.

"Who is that?" Marnie asked as Justin stepped out of the house.

Jesse turned and looked at Justin, who she had to admit looked great on her porch. She felt her face flush and hoped Marnie hadn't seen it.

Justin had been surprised when he woke to an empty bed. It was usually he who ran off early in the morning before the girl woke up, not wanting to face the commitments of the new day. He had rolled over to kiss Jess good morning but instead had come face to face with a fluffy pillow that smelled just like vanilla and apples. He found himself beginning to love that smell.

For some strange reason he found himself eager to see Jesse and see how she was doing this morning. He knew she had a hard day ahead of her with burying Cozy and all the searching they were going to do in town.

After getting dressed and running a hand through his hair he headed for the kitchen. Not at all surprised to see no one there, he headed out to the barn. The air felt so good against his face that he hadn't realized how long he had stood there soaking up its warmth and strength until he caught a glimpse of Jesse talking to another woman.

"Oh him, he's, ah…" Jesse stumbled for the words. "Logan's grandson."

"You mean the caretaker?" Marnie hadn't missed the sudden loss of words Jess had; she knew her friend too well not to know that Jess had feelings for this guy. He was coming out of her house and looking like he hadn't seen the day yet. Marnie had to admit he was handsome.

"Yes."

"Why is he at your house? That is your house, isn't it?"

"Yes it is. But everybody eats over here."

"Yeah, right." She smiled a knowing smile at Jesse, whose smile broadened. She knew Marnie had her figured out.

"Oh be quiet, Marnie, we didn't do anything. I had a rough night and he was a shoulder to cry on, that's all."

Marnie's face dropped. "What happened last night to make you cry?" Marnie knew very well if Jess cried it was a serious reason. She had always been so proud of Jesse's strength when it came to sad movies or stories. She cried at the drop of a hat, but not Jess.

Jesse could feel her eyes growing moist as she thought about how to put what happened into words for Marnie.

"I told you about the strange people up here."

"Yes. What did they do, Jess?"

"They killed..." A new batch of tears came to her eyes and she couldn't finish the story.

Justin could see Jesse's shoulders slump from where he stood on the porch. He knew she was telling the young woman with blond hair about Cozy. He figured it was Marnie, but he was drawn to Jesse as she stood there in all her sorrow. He made quick work of the distance between Jesse and the house, and as he came up beside her he placed an arm around her shoulders.

Jesse was thankful for the warmth of Justin's arms.

"They killed who?" Marnie asked, suddenly worried and not at all interested in the man that held Jesse in his arms.

"They killed Cozy," Justin stated, and was shocked to see Marnie's eyes fill with tears as well. She looked as lost as Jesse.

"How could anyone kill him? He was the sweetest horse ever. Oh, Jesse dear, I am so sorry." Marnie flung her arms around Jesse's shoulders. Justin stepped back and watched as the two stood in the comfort of each other's embrace, and tears ran down both women's cheeks. They stood for what seemed like forever until the tears stopped running and then they parted and wiped their eyes.

Justin smiled at the closeness of the two friends. It was obvious that Marnie and Jesse were very good friends. He knew friends like that were hard to find.

"Are these the other three broodmares, Jess?" Justin asked, breaking the silence.

"Oh yes, they are."

"I will see to them if you two want to go get caught up with each other."

"Thank you. That would be great."

"Remember to inform her about what we're doing today."

"You mean going into town?" Jess asked, and Justin nodded.

Marnie brazenly stepped forward, wiping the tears from her eyes. "Jess has horrible manners some days. I'm Marnie, and you are?"

"Justin. I figured you were Marnie, Jesse said you were coming up today."

Opening the trailer, Justin untied the mares and headed them to the pasture. He turned and watched Jesse and Marnie make their way to the house with Marnie's bags. He knew he was going to enjoy escorting those two around town tonight. He was going to be envied by all who saw him with those two beautiful women.

Once inside the house, Marnie dropped the bags she was carrying and turned to Jesse.

"Okay, fess up. Are you two doing anything I should know about?"

"Like what, Marnie?" Jesse knew what she was asking but she wasn't about to explain anything to her, at least not yet.

"You know darn well what I'm talking about. So are you?"

"No. We don't have that kind of relationship."

"Oh, all right then. Is he free?"

"No, not really." Jesse knew her smile was giving her away but she didn't care. The last few days had been too horrible and she wanted to confide her feelings for Justin to someone, preferably her best friend.

"So I'm right after all, you do like him."

"Yes, I do like him, but he likes me one moment and hates me the next. He hates me because I know Jack and because Jack likes me, even though I want nothing to do with Jack."

"Jack is your old high school boyfriend, right?"

"Yes, but he has been trying to ignite an old flame that was never there. And with all the killing of cattle and Cozy and even Justin's dog, Jinks, I don't know who to trust, but I do know that I trust Justin."

"So you haven't kissed him yet?"

"Ooh boy. Have we done that. You know, between you, me, and those stupid cows you keep giving me, I'm not sure what I ever saw in Hank."

"Did you get your papers filed for the divorce?" Marnie asked.

"Yes. I did that the other day."

"Good. Now that we're all caught up, where is this store that I get to work in? I want to see it right away."

"I wish we could run down there but I promised Justin we would go to town and see if I recognize any voices from last night."

"You mean you were close enough to hear someone?"

"Yes. Unfortunately, I heard two guys. I know I can recognize them by their voices if I ever hear them again. One sounded really familiar but I couldn't put a name to it."

Suddenly Jesse stopped; her face fell. Marnie could tell something was wrong.

"Jesse, what is it? What's wrong?"

"I do know whose voice that was, but it can't be true."

Jesse ran from the house yelling Justin's name as she headed towards the barn. She knew exactly who one voice belonged to, but she couldn't believe it to be true. How could she have not recognized it last night? Marnie was right on her heels as she entered the barn. Justin heard her screams and ran towards her from the fawn's stall.

"Justin!"

"What is it, Jess?" Justin questioned. As they met face-to-face he could tell by her expression that it was serious.

"I know who that voice belonged to."

"What? Whose is it?"

"I didn't recognize it at first, though I don't know how come I didn't."

Justin was losing his patience.

"Whose is it, Jess?"

"Jack's! I know it was Jack's."

"Are you sure?"

"The lady at the drugstore said there was a Jack Love. Do you think maybe it was him?"

"I wouldn't put it past him. What do you want to do?"

"Come on, let's go see him."

"I don't want to go, Jess," Marnie stated. "I'll go to the store or just stay here. I don't want to catch a murderer no matter how much I loved Cozy."

"That's all right, Marnie, I understand. I would feel better if you go over to Mary and Logan's house and wait for us to get back."

"I can do that." With that, she turned and walked towards the bunkhouse to introduce herself and stay with Mary and Logan.

"Let's take my truck," Justin said. In a matter of minutes they were heading towards Jack's parents' old ranch to take another look at the bay gelding. After Jess told Justin about him, they realized that was most likely how he was able to get up on the range to shoot at them.

The drive over found Jesse and Justin discussing Jack's behavior and how they should have at least thought of him being responsible for all of this a little bit. Jesse knew she was going to see him prosecuted to the full extent when she found him and had him convicted of Cozy's death.

"Jesse, why doesn't your husband know you still have the ranch?" Justin questioned. That statement had bothered him last night. Why hadn't Jesse's husband known of the Running W? According to Logan they had gotten married right after the death of Jess's parents and they left the ranch to her. She had to have told him about being left the ranch.

"I never told Hank about being left the ranch. In fact I told him my parents had sold it to pay for some debt they had acquired through the years."

"Why did you tell him that?"

"Hank wasn't a very nice person, and had he known my parents left me the ranch, he would have wanted to move back here. He would have squandered away the cattle and any money I could have made. I never even told him about the insurance money, instead I bought Boe and told him they had left him to me."

"Didn't you trust him?"

"Not with money, his or mine."

"Sounds like he was a bit self-centered. Logan talks about him every now and then and says he was arrogant."

"That's putting it nicely." Jesse figured now was as good a time as any to find out about Justin's history. "What about your love life? You said once you would tell me about it."

"Well, she sounds a lot like Hank. In fact they sound perfect for one another. Annie was her name. She was nice and caring from the beginning until my parents died and left me with a little bit of money."

"So you are rich?" Jesse laughed at the fact that they both were hiding the same secret.

"I'm okay."

"And then she wasn't so nice anymore?"

"Yeah, pretty much."

"Were you engaged?"

"Not really. I guess. I gave her a really nice diamond ring and asked her to marry me and she threw it back at me and told me I could afford better."

"Wow, what a bitch."

"Yeah. Well, she taught me a lot about women."

"So is that why you don't want a commitment?"

"That's part of it."

"What is the other part?"

"Oh, we don't have to talk about it right now. We have both been treated pretty badly by previous partners, let's just leave it at that."

"I meant what I said last night, Justin. I'm not Annie and I know what it feels like to not trust your other half." That was all she could say; she knew if she said more her voice would show the still painful gap that Hank had left in her confidence in being worth loving.

"I will hold you to it one day."

Jesse was so caught up in thoughts of the past that she had almost forgotten what she had said he was going to hold her to.

"What?"

"You know what."

Jesse blushed as she remembered their agreement.

They turned into the old Smith place and drove straight to the barn. Jesse jumped out and charged into the barn and straight to where she saw the bay stalled. Justin was right behind her.

As she turned to the stall, the sight was not what she had expected. The stall was empty, but horse droppings were still scattered on the stall floor.

"I swear he was right here."

"I believe you, Jess. The manure is still rather fresh. I would say maybe last night at the latest. Come on, let's look around a little bit, maybe he got worried and moved him someplace else."

"Of course, I said I saw his horse last night. He said it wasn't his and he also said he was going to check on the place last night."

They walked up and down the aisles and looked around every nook and cranny. There was no sign of Jack or the bay gelding. They stood at the entrance looking out towards the open fields.

"Oh well, I guess he must have moved him. Should we be heading to Republic so we can confront him at work?"

"Probably."

"Damn birds," Jesse muttered as something wet hit her arm. She looked down to see a bright red spot on her arm.

"What the heck?" She suddenly looked up and screamed.

Following her attention, Justin looked up to see a large gunnysack dangling from the outside overhang. The bottom of the sack was soaked in blood.

Chapter 15

Justin told her, "I'm going to call the police. My cell phone is in the pickup." He ran to the pickup, phoned the police, and retold the scene. He hung up and returned to Jesse's side by the water trough, where she was busy trying to wash off the blood.

"They're on their way. Are you okay?"

"Not really. What do you think is in there?"

"I don't know, but if I had to guess I would say maybe your bay gelding's head that you saw."

"What is wrong with Jack? Why would he do this?"

"I don't know why he would do this or anything else he has done."

"I know I made him mad when I left with Hank but we talked about it for some time the other day. He said he was mad at me at first but then he got over it."

"You left Jack for Hank? I didn't know you were very serious about Jack when you were dating him."

"I wasn't. I mean we were serious for kids, I guess. We held hands and that kind of stuff but we never did anything farther."

Justin didn't realize he had been holding his breath until he released it. In the back of his mind, he had already convinced himself that she had slept with him sometime during her life. To hear otherwise gave him a renewed faith in women for maybe what was the first time in his life.

Despite the situation, Jesse wanted to laugh at the look on Justin's face. It was a mixture of humor, gratitude, and shock. Justin must have thought she and Jack had been screwing.

"You know, your faith in me is astounding."

"What do you mean?"

"You thought I slept with him. Didn't you?"

"No, the thought never even crossed my mind." He wasn't about to let her have the satisfaction of knowing she had that much effect on him. Or the fact that the thought of those two together had been torturing him ever since that day they had lunch at the café.

"Tell the truth." She was moving towards him as a cat would move towards a mouse. She knew he was lying and so did he.

"Fine, miss know-it-all, yes, I did think that. But, I'll bet you thought the same thing about Karla and me. In fact I know you did."

"You're absolutely right, Justin. I was terribly jealous when you and Karla kissed that night after Logan and Mary dropped us off."

"What kiss? Oh, you mean that. Karla kissed me, I never returned the kiss. Not like with..." He stopped and looked at her. She knew what he was thinking.

"Like with me."

"Yes."

The sound of sirens brought them back to the reality of the situation at hand. They watched as two police cars drove up and parked by Justin's pickup truck.

One said "Police Department" down the side, the other just read "Sheriff." The deputy from that morning stepped out and looked at them as if to say hello again.

The other car's door swung open to reveal a large man with a barrel chest, his uniform snug around his chest and waist. As he stood, Jesse had to make note of the sheer height of the man; he must be well over six foot and well built. She doubted there was an ounce of fat on the big man.

"You two are finding a lot of trouble lately, I hear," the large man stated with a wry grin.

"Are you the sheriff?" Jesse asked.

"I am, but not from this county. Seems Sheriff Morris had to go somewhere, so they called me in from the next county over. I'm Sheriff Conrad."

"The sack up there is dripping with blood." Justin motioned towards the ceiling of the barn.

"Deputy, climb up in that loft and retrieve that bag, would you?"

"Yes, Sheriff." With that said, the overweight deputy disappeared inside the barn only to reappear some time later out of breath and sweating profusely up in the loft. "How do I get the sack down, Sheriff?"

"Just let it drop. Whatever is in there is already dead."

The mere thought of that made Jesse cringe. Justin wrapped a protective arm around her. She turned her face into his shoulder as the bag made a lunge towards earth with a horrible thud. The sheriff immediately walked towards it in a slow, cautious way.

He knelt down and touched the red stain on the sack. A quick glance back up towards the deputy told his thoughts. A quick motion of his hand revealed a knife, with which he cut the sack open carefully. Jesse screamed as an arm fell free, followed by a head and torso.

"Jack!" Jesse screamed.

The sheriff turned his attention towards Jesse.

"You know this man?"

"Yes I do. He was a friend of mine. That was, until I thought he killed my horse, Cozy. I was sure I recognized his voice from last night. I remembered seeing a big bay gelding over here the other day. I put two and two together and I was sure it was him."

"Well, if that's true, maybe the other guy got mad at him and did him in," the big sheriff said.

Her explanation sounded more like an apology, but she couldn't help it. She had known deep down she was wrong, and had accused Jack of something he could not have done. He had never been cruel or rude even after he had learned of her leaving with Hank.

Now he was dead and it was probably because of her. If she had not told him about the bay gelding in his barn he would not have set foot on this place, and probably would not have been murdered. The cold hard facts of it were that it was her fault, and he was inside that sack. She knew it, even if no one else would say it.

Jesse could feel her eyes misting over. Maybe her best bet was just to go away again. First someone shot at her and Justin, then killed Cozy and Jinks, and now Jack. It was almost as if someone was after her. She turned her head towards Justin—maybe he was next on the list, or Mary, or Logan. There was no way she would forgive herself if all this was because of her.

The stress of the day must have been getting to her. Justin had said bad things were happening before she showed up. One thing was for sure: come Wednesday she was going to be seated in a chair at the Anti-Love Organization's weekly meeting.

After answering a few more of the sheriff's questions, both Justin and Jesse headed back to the ranch. The ride was silent. Their minds raced over whats, ifs, and whos. It was Justin who finally broke the silence.

"Jesse, you do know we're going to have to try to figure this out. Someone is killing our friends, cows, and other animals. We are going to have to get to the bottom of it even if it costs us some more lives."

Jesse knew what he was saying was true. She had been thinking the same thing since the discovery of Jack's body.

"How do we go about it?"

"I think we need to start back up at Golden Water Pond."

"What? Why there?"

"Well, because he must have spent some time up on the cliffs watching us. Maybe he dropped something or left us a clue. He shot at us so maybe he left a spent cartridge. He watched us split up and stayed until he shot at us; that had to have been a good half an hour or so that he was there. Maybe we could even pick up a horse track."

"Good idea. When do we leave?"

"Tomorrow morning after breakfast."

"I guess I'll ride Boe tomorrow. I will miss riding Cozy, he was so well broke. I never spent the time training Boe as well because he was a stallion."

"I have a big buckskin gelding you can try out if you want to. He's nicely broke."

"What's his name?"

"Why, don't think I can name anything?"

"When I said we should name the fawn, you're the one who said you can't name anything."

"His name is Montana. We call him Monty for short."

"Not bad. Who named him?"

"Boy, do you have a lot of questions when someone offers you a gelding to ride."

"Sorry, I just didn't want to ride a horse your girlfriend Karla named." Jesse couldn't help but poke fun at Justin a little.

"I am going to return that one hundred percent. Nobody teases me and gets away with it."

It felt good teasing and joking around with each other after what had taken place in their lives in the last four days. Justin couldn't help but compare Jesse to Annie. He didn't mean to, but guessed it was natural to compare an old love to a newfound friend.

Annie had always been so proper and regal in public. She never let her cool exterior fall in front of any peers. Jesse couldn't care less what other people thought of her appearance. Money had been Annie's main goal in life. Jesse's seemed to revolve around a good horse and her friends.

Both were beautiful in every aspect. Jesse was a lot taller and her skin was already tanned from the few days of sun this year had already supplied them with. Annie would have never allowed herself to tan. She used to comment on women who did and state that they looked like field hands.

Looking back now, he couldn't remember what he saw in Annie. She wasn't his type at all; she didn't ride horses or care about the outdoors. Maybe he was wrong for hating her all these years. Maybe he should be thanking her for showing her true colors then and not waiting until they were married and had children together.

"So who did name him, Justin?" Jesse's voice broke his thoughts.

"Logan actually named him. He was the nicest of our first foals, so we kept him as a prospect and he's a good gelding. He's six years old, looks a lot like Badger in stature. But he's a lot more social, and he doesn't get quite the attention anymore."

"Why not?"

"Well, I have Badger and I don't want another horse, so I broke him and turned him out, but he wouldn't have changed much. I was going to sell him about two years ago when I started Badger, but Logan wouldn't let me do it."

"I'm glad. I can't wait to meet him." With that Jesse turned and looked out the window as they pulled into the drive. She saw Marnie and Mary sitting on the porch steps of Jesse's house drinking a glass of something and chatting.

She knew once Mary and Marnie met they were going to get along fine. Marnie had always been an easy person to know. Jesse thought of the many times she had been less than fun to hang around with and still Marnie forgave her for being cruel or less than thoughtful.

She was pleased that Marnie had decided to come and stay at the ranch. They were bound to have so much fun around there as soon as they found who was responsible for all the killings. Then they could turn their attention to all the fun stuff they could do. Marnie had never wanted to learn to ride back in Caldwell, but now Jesse bet she could get her to learn to ride.

Jesse stepped from the truck and gave a see-you-later smile to Justin; she guessed he must have understood.

"Meet me out at the barn about ten o'clock tonight, would you?" Justin asked.

"Okay, on the dot." With that, she turned and walked towards Mary and Marnie. She knew Mary wasn't going to like to hear the news she was bringing with her about Jack's murder. But she guessed she had to tell her; she was going to find out one way or another. It was too small of a town not to find out about another murder.

As she approached, she could hear Mary telling Marnie about her when she was a child and about how wild she had been.

"Mary?" Jesse said as she sat down on the step below her.

"Yes, Jessica, what is it?" Mary could read Jesse's worried looks. She had them a lot when she was a kid and did something wrong but didn't want to tell her parents, so she would sit on

Mary's front porch steps just like she was now and have that same worried frown on her face.

"Justin and I went to the old Smith homestead today."

"Oh, I heard it was pretty run down but I haven't been over there since the Smiths moved."

"Yeah, it's pretty run down. But something happened over there that I need to tell you about."

"What is it?" Mary knew it was serious by the look on Jessica's face, but she couldn't guess why she was beating around the bush about telling her.

"We found a body over there." Mary and Marnie both gasped at the news.

"Oh my goodness, who was it?" Mary's fear was suddenly evident.

"It was Jack," Jesse solemnly revealed.

"Oh, that's terrible news. Are you okay?" Marnie inquired.

"Yes, I guess so. I will be a lot better when all of this stops."

"Was it the same as the others?" Jesse knew Mary was asking if he was murdered.

"Yes it was, pretty much." She didn't feel a reason to reveal all the gruesome details of the day.

"Poor Jack. I had better go find Logan and inform him." Jesse watched as Mary stood and made haste for the barns.

"Isn't that your friend?" Marnie questioned.

"Yes, he was my friend a long time ago, and he was beginning to be my friend again until this happened." Jesse wondered if she should tell Marnie about Justin and her idea on trying to get to the bottom of all this by themselves. But she decided not to since she knew Marnie would try to talk her out of it.

"Mary informed me about everything that has been going on here lately. I'm very worried. What are you going to do?"

"Do? What can I do, Marnie?"

"Well I know you won't leave, so to suggest that would just make you mad. How about the police, aren't they doing anything?"

"No, they aren't, and it seems the whole town is run by these people called Love, their last names are all Love."

"Hey, just like that cult down in California I read about." Marnie remembered the article well—it had made her skin crawl when she read it some years back. To think of it now gave her that same feeling.

"Tell me what you remember."

"I remember it all. These guys were stealing children, mostly little girls, and raising them in this cult-like environment. They were changing their names to weird things like Faith Love, Special Love, Windy Love, and so on. They would raise them without any rules of society but the cult's. They didn't abide by the government's laws at all. And the top man at the time was Chance Love. He struck me as a real jerk."

"How long ago was this?"

"Eleven, twelve years ago, one of the children escaped and told all of this to the newspaper. I can't remember her name though."

"Do you think the story would be on the Internet somewhere?"

"I don't know why it wouldn't. I could go check on my laptop if you have a hookup."

"I know Mary and Logan do. I have to go take care of a few things. I won't be in till late if that's all right." Jesse still had to go bury Cozy and then go meet with Justin.

"I'll be fine. I'll just hang out with Mary. I like her a lot."

"I knew you would like her when you met her. I'll see you in the morning, Marnie."

"Okay." She ran into the house to get her laptop and head to Mary and Logan's. Jesse stood up and walked to the barn to get Cozy's bridle and go say goodbye to an old friend.

Chapter 16

She was glad to see Logan had found a beautiful spot to bury him. There was a view of the Canadian slopes in the distance and two big trees on either side of the coffin. Logan still had the coffin sitting next to the hole. The large box had an engraving on the side, which Jesse had to kneel down to read.

Cozy
Every good cowboy or cowgirl is only granted
one good dog and one great horse a lifetime
and now a good dog I must find.
An Unknown Cowboy

She smiled. Logan had said those words many times to her, at least a shortened version of them. He would always tell her that she is granted only one good horse and one good dog in a lifetime so make them count and keep an eye out for the other.

Jesse opened the lid just enough to slide Cozy's bridle in and not enough to see him.

"My dear sweet friend, you were the best horse I shall ever own and every horse from now on will be only compared to you."

Jesse was thinking to herself about all the days and years she had spent with him and how he had changed her life. She didn't even hear Logan as he stepped up behind her.

"Jessica, Mary told me about Jack. That's too bad. He was a nice boy." Jesse nodded.

"Logan, I want to find these guys responsible and make sure justice finds them one way or another. I know you aren't going to approve, but Marnie thinks she might remember a newspaper clipping about a cult down in California that sounds just like what I have heard about this one."

"What have you heard about this one?"

"That a group of people who all have the same last name, Love, moved in and are taking over the towns of Republic and Danville and who knows where else. Even the mayor's last name is Love. Maybe the police are in on it as well. I know that a lot of good people and animals are dying for no good reason, and—" Jesse stopped and thought of what else she knew.

"And what else, Jessica?"

"And I'm going to the Anti-Love Organization meeting next Wednesday and I'm going to get all the information I can about them." Jesse's blood was heating up just talking about it.

"Sounds like you have a game plan already. Let me know if I can help."

"What? That's it? You aren't going to try to stop me?"

Jesse couldn't believe it.

"Nope, I ain't. They killed your horse. Where I'm from that means revenge. I will bury him tonight for you if you would like me to."

"Yes, that would be great, thanks." Jesse watched as Logan turned and strode back to his house. Sometimes people amazed her in their actions, but he seemed to amaze her all the time.

Jesse knew she would have to have a small marker made for him some day soon, but right now she had to go meet Justin. It was almost dark and she knew Justin would worry if she was late, but first she had to get the information Marnie had found so she could relay it to Justin.

Jesse wondered how much revenge she was allowed to unleash on these people before Logan called it enough. She knew she couldn't just pick up a rope and a gun and go to killing. Danville wasn't that far out in the hills.

Marnie had a large stack of papers lying on the computer bench when Jesse arrived back at Logan's house. Marnie's nose was stuck on the computer screen.

"Her name was Grace Jenkins. She was originally from San Francisco, California. They had her for three years before she escaped."

"Three years? Could you do a people search and find her new address?"

"Yes, I probably could, why?"

"Well, if we can find her then maybe we can have her identify some photos of the people around here. And if that works then we should be able to get the FBI in here to help clear this all up."

"Yes, I think you're right. Good idea, Jess. You know, I feel like one of those women in my books, or like Sherlock Holmes."

"Do I get to be Watson?"

Marnie giggled a little as she punched in some more numbers and letters on the keyboard. Soon a picture and an address for Grace Jenkins came up in front of them.

"That's her?" Jesse asked. The woman in front of them didn't look like a victim. She looked carefree and pretty. Her blond hair fell in front of her narrow shoulders and her blue eyes looked like they held the answer to a thousand mysteries, one of which Jesse wanted the answers to.

"That's her. Grace Ann Jenkins, age twenty-seven years."

"How old was she when she was abducted?"

"Well she was fifteen when they found her, and she had been with them for three years prior, so she was twelve when they took her."

"I have to go meet Justin. Would you print all her information out for me?"

"Sure. I also printed out the newspaper article. I didn't read all of it, but it was just as I remembered. You two will have to read it all the way through."

"We can do that." When Marnie had handed her the last few pieces of paper she thanked her again and headed to the barn to meet Justin.

When she entered the barn, she found Justin watering Badger and Maggie.

"Hey, you're early, Jess."

"Disappointed?"

"Never. Do you want to talk here?"

"Let's go to your place, Justin. It's getting kind of cold and anyway I have some papers we have to read, so it will be nice to spread them out on a table."

"You're the boss, Boss. What kind of papers do you have that we need to read?"

"I'll explain on the way over, and don't call me boss." Jesse hated to stand around chatting when someone could so easily be listening in on their conversation or lining them up in the crosshairs. Besides, she didn't like to look at the stall where Cozy had been. It made her sad all over again.

They loaded into Justin's truck and headed to his house. She explained what Marnie had told her and how she had found the article on the Internet. She also told him about the girl and what had happened to her and where she was now and that they had found her address.

Justin listened intently to the story as he drove. When at last they pulled up in front of his house, Jesse cringed in memory of the last time she was here. She didn't think she could ever look at this place without thinking of that night. It was by far the worst night of her whole life.

"Come on in," Justin invited her.

"After you." As they entered, Jesse could see he had a new fridge. She figured he must have sent away for it because he had been at work every single hour since and it seemed so soon to already have a new fridge.

"I see you have a new fridge already." Jesse hadn't meant to say anything, but her curiosity of how he got it so quickly was beginning to make her nervous.

"Yes. I had that one out in the shop. So I moved it into the house. Go ahead and sit on the couch, Jesse. Spread your papers out on the coffee table. I'm going to get a beer, do you want one?"

"Yeah, I guess it sounds okay."

"I don't have any popcorn to go with it."

"Well I guess we'll have to make due for now."

After downing a couple beers and talking about what Marnie had found on the Internet, Jesse had Justin up to date on what she knew.

"So you and Marnie think we should call in the FBI and get them to bust this ring?" Justin had to admit it wasn't a bad idea to bring in outside agents who had nothing to do with the town or any of its residents.

"First we will have to go to the Anti-Love Organization and get all the information they have and then we have to get as many photos of them as we possibly can. One of us three will have to fly to California and get Grace Jenkins to identify them in front of the FBI."

"Not me, I have to stay here, and you had better as well. It's probably safer for Marnie if you let her go." Justin didn't want to come right out and say that there was no way in hell he was going to allow her to leave the ranch without him. If she decided to go to California herself he was just going to have to tag along to make sure she didn't come to any harm.

He knew he was thinking a lot like a jealous boyfriend again but he didn't care. To Justin's relief, Jesse agreed that Marnie was the best person to go.

"So are we supposed to read all these papers you brought over?" Justin asked, looking at the stack of papers spread out on his coffee table.

"They're all about Grace Jenkins and the Love cult that abducted her. I think we should know what we're up against." Jesse knew it looked like a long night of reading, but she just had to know what happened to Grace Jenkins when she was abducted.

"Well, I guess we had better get started."

They each took a handful of papers and went to reading. Jesse was horrified. Grace was just twelve years old when she was taken from her summer camp. Surprisingly, no one knew she was missing until fifteen days later.

Jesse found that strange. When she had gone to summer camp they counted heads every night when they called lights out.

"Justin, did you ever go to a summer camp?"

"No, why?"

"No one noticed she was gone for fifteen days. Isn't that strange?"

"Yeah, I guess. But they probably had a lot of kids to worry about."

"Maybe you're right, but still it sounds a little funky to me. Can I use your phone?"

"Yeah, it's on the wall by the fridge."

Jesse called Marnie. After two rings, Marnie answered, "Walker's ranch. This is Marnie."

"Marnie, it's Jess. Did you ever go to any camp other than 4-H camp?"

"Yes, I went to Lake Jade's camp for girls," Marnie said.

"Did they do head checks before you went to bed at night?" Jesse asked.

"Yes, and when we ate breakfast every morning."

"That's what I thought. Will you check out this camp that Grace Jenkins was taken from? They didn't know she was missing for fifteen days. Also, will you check out camp policy on head checks see if it is mandatory in every state?"

"Yes, I'll run over to Mary and Logan's and check it out right now. Oh, and I have some exciting news for you. I just got off the phone with Grace Jenkins."

"You talked to her? What did she say?"

"She said that she would love to help us catch them in any way she can. So I told her I was going to email some photos to her in the next few days. But Mary overheard me talking to her and she said that the mayor has a website with his photos on it, or so she was told. So I typed in 'Republic Mayor Love' and guess what popped up?"

"I have no clue."

"His campaign speech. Five times within one ten-minute speech he said, 'I will make you all one with me.' I find that odd. But what is odder is that he won 434 to 107. You know what that means, don't you?"

"That there are four hundred and thirty-four 'Love' members in or around this area?"

"That's what I was thinking as well, but I sent the photo to Grace and am now awaiting her email or call to tell me if she recognizes him."

"We'll come over in a couple hours. I want to finish the newspaper article first."

"There's no hurry. It could take her hours to get back to me. I'm going to have dinner with Mary and Logan, and Mary has insisted that I stay here until you get home."

"We shouldn't be very long."

"You two have fun."

"Funny, Marnie." Jesse hung up the phone and turned to Justin.

"Thank goodness for modern technology. It looks like we won't have to go to California after all. Marnie called and talked to Grace Jenkins and she is now trying to see if the mayor is one of them."

"That's great news. Are we supposed to head over pretty quick?"

"Yes, in a couple hours or so. Hey, did you know that Mayor Love won his campaign on a speech that involved making you 'one with him'?"

"No, I never follow politics. Why do you find that so odd?"

"In one ten-minute speech Marnie said he repeated that phrase five times."

"Five times? Why, that would be almost his whole speech."

"That's what I was thinking. Do you know of any missing children or young women around here since they moved in?"

"Well, I think there's been about six or seven, and quite a few deaths or bodies found. You think it's all tied together? You know, if that is true, we are way in over our heads."

"Yeah, I know. But what do we do?"

"Hide our heads under the covers and never come out again." Jesse laughed.

"That would entail you and me under the covers together, Jess, you think that's a good idea?"

"No. Not right now. I don't." Jesse knew she was leading him on and she wasn't able to finish what she started. God only knew how much she wanted to jump under the covers with Justin and forget everything that was going on.

"Maybe later, after all this is over for good."

"What if it's never over?" Jesse smiled at Justin's boyish attempts to lighten the subject.

"Well then, I guess we will never know."

"Know what, Jess?"

"Know if you are as good as you think you are."

Justin closed the distance between them in one stride. He placed his hand at the base of Jesse's neck and pulled her towards him until his mouth claimed hers in a quick but meaningful kiss.

"I am, and I don't have to have you under the covers for you to know that."

"Not to change the subject, but we have to finish the article and get over to Logan and Mary's. Plus we have to get up nice and early tomorrow so that you can introduce me to Monty and we can go up to Golden Meadow."

"Okay, you win," Justin said. The last time they went up there they had been shot at.

Jesse had no clue what she had just won. She hadn't intended to win anything. She wanted Justin's kisses more than an almost divorced woman should want, but she also wanted to find the murderers and see them locked behind bars for a very long time. She also knew that if she started kissing Justin they weren't going to get anything accomplished anytime soon.

The past few days seemed to have flown by. Half the time she didn't know if she was coming or going and the other half she was sure if she was losing her mind in every sense of the word.

"Well, let's get over and find out if Marnie found out anything new. I need sleep."

"Sounds good. Come on, let's get going."

They barely spoke on the ride back. Both of their heads were spinning about all the new facts they had learned about Grace Jenkins and the Loves. They had a lot of work ahead of them.

Once in the comfort of Mary and Logan's kitchen, Marnie was happy to reveal the news about Grace verifying Mayor Love as one of the ones who had kidnapped her.

"So we got them?" Marnie happily exclaimed.

"Not yet, Marnie. There is still the question of why they are picking on this ranch in particular," Logan added in.

"You're right, Logan, it has all been pointing towards us lately. Even Jack is a direct link to us by way of Jesse." Mary knew she was only stating the obvious, but it didn't matter.

"Marnie, are you sure you never said anything to Hank before you left? Or anyone who would talk to Hank?" Jesse asked.

"I never said anything to anybody. I told work I was quitting to move to Florida to take care of my Aunt Bethany."

"I can't help it. It's almost like Hank is somehow behind all of this. This Love cult thing is definitely throwing me off. What did you find out about that camp, Marnie?"

"Camp regulations state a head count has to made at least once a day."

"And who owned the camp?"

"Camp Love Thy Neighbor was owned by none other than a man called Kurt Love and his lovely wife Faith Love."

"Of course it was. Who else would it be owned by?" Jesse was concerned that this Love group was a lot bigger than she thought it was.

"There's a Faith Love in Republic."

"But we found out a lot more. After Grace Jenkins went missing, the camp closed down and no one has been able to track down Kurt or Faith Love. The Anti-Love Organization has a website in Republic; it's an organization against all Loves, as far as I can tell."

"I know about it. I talked to a lady who heads up this organization. She said there are seventy-seven members in this county right now."

"That may be, Jess, but it's bigger than just this county. I explained some of what I knew was going on around here to their forums and I got sixty emails about these people, and most sent an album of photos. All we have to do is confirm it is the same group."

"Marnie, you are awesome." Justin smiled at her. He couldn't believe she had done so much research in such a short time.

"I hope you don't mind but I'm going to do some investigating at your store over the next few days. I think I can use your surveillance cameras and get still photos of them, but I can also check driver's licenses of anyone I suspect as being one of them."

"Marnie, I never knew you were a mystery type of woman."

"Me neither, Jess, but this is fun."

Jesse had known Marnie as being a very fragile woman, not a tough one who had no fear of death or worse. This new Marnie impressed her. Her hair was up in a clip, and her glasses were low on her nose. Maybe Jesse had never really known the real Marnie.

Chapter 17

The next morning Jesse was shocked to be awakened to the sound of a knock on her bedroom door. It was still dark outside. After a quick look at her clock she realized it was only four in the morning. She stumbled from bed and opened the door and was shocked to see Justin standing there, his eyes focused on a piece of paper in his hands. When he looked up she saw a strange, confused look.

"Justin, what's wrong?"

"This was on the front window of my truck this morning as I got ready to come to work." He handed her the note.

Jesse quickly read it.

Asshole,

Leave Jess alone, she is not for you, next time the bullet won't miss if you try to screw her. But if I were you I would move far away and never look back.

Love

"Oh my god, it has to be Hank."

"That's what I was thinking. I want you to call him and see if he's home." She walked to the window, closed the curtains, and motioned for Justin to sit down in the chair.

"All right." Jesse picked up the phone and dialed her old number. After three rings a man picked up the receiver.

"Hello?"

Jesse quickly hung up the phone. There was no mistaking Hank's voice. That was Hank for sure.

"He's home, Justin. It couldn't be him," Jesse said, almost relieved. Justin quickly stood and closed the distance between them.

"Jesse, you have to think who would want me to stay away from you and why."

"Jack and Hank are the only two I can think of. Jack is dead and Hank is in Caldwell."

"Can you think of anyone else who would want you for themselves?" Justin asked.

"Justin, you have to leave. You have to take Logan and Mary and Marnie too and just go away and let whoever this is kill me without hurting anyone else."

Jesse collapsed into Justin's arms. Justin couldn't believe what she had just said. There was no way he was going to let anything happen to her.

"Don't talk crazy, Jess. I couldn't leave you even if I wanted to. I am here beside you until we figure this out or get ourselves killed trying."

"So you're committed to helping me?"

"Yes I am."

"But I thought commitment wasn't your thing?"

"It wasn't. Isn't! But with you, I see hope."

Justin looked down into her worry-filled green eyes and ached to know how to erase all that worry. His lips slowly found their way to hers. He knew this was going to get him in trouble, but he didn't care. He wanted to be close to her right now and right there.

Jesse quickly responded to Justin's hot and tempting kisses. Jesse wrapped both arms around Justin's neck and pressed her body full length to his.

Justin's low moan let Jesse know her effect on him. Without warning, Justin swept her up in his arms and placed her on the bed, then laid down beside her. His body molded against hers. His breath was hot as he kissed her neck and moved down to the hollow of her collarbone.

Jesse threw her head back at the sheer force of his kisses. Her body quivered, and an ache of wanting desire rose in her stomach and pooled there, warming her insides to boiling temperature.

"Justin, I think..." Justin cut her off with a deep kiss.

"Stop thinking, just make love to me."

"I can do that," she said, and she did.

The morning sun was warm as it shone in through the open curtains and kissed Justin and Jesse's naked entangled limbs.

Justin woke and stared down into the angel's face in his arms. He never believed he would ever care for a woman again, but it happened, and he had to admit to himself and to no one else that he desperately loved Jesse.

He didn't know what today, tomorrow, or the next day might bring, but if this was his last day on earth, he knew he was going to die a very happy man.

Jesse felt so right in his arms, and he hated to wake her and get the day started, but he knew he was going to have to do it sooner or later.

He bent his head and scattered soft kisses across her brow. Jesse stirred and moaned a low, seductive sound. Justin felt his body stir to life. It was hard to believe a sound could bring his body to such full awareness of his need for her.

"Justin?"

"Yes, Jess, what is it?"

"Do I have to get up and face yet another day of this junk? I'm definitely having second thoughts about 'love' as well."

"Why is that?"

"Why couldn't those people pick a different last name? I'm down on love anyway and now I hate it that much more."

"You know, for a second I thought this conversation was headed somewhere else." Justin was afraid she was having second thoughts about what they had done a few hours before.

"No, that was fine."

"Just fine?"

"Well I was pretty dang good, wasn't I?"

"You're so funny, Jess, but as a matter of fact you weren't bad."

"I know, but enough about me. We had better get up and head out if we are going to get to the meadow and check things out."

"Did you still want to go see Bill?"

"Yes, I almost forgot. So thanks for reminding me. The other day when I had lunch with Jack I went in to say hi to him and he couldn't or wouldn't talk to me because someone was in the back. He didn't want them to know he knew me."

"Maybe that's the person we're looking for. If he didn't want them to know he knew you personally, maybe there was a reason, like they were asking about you."

"You know what? All these things are starting to come together. But what if Hank is behind all of this? He does have some friends still up in this area."

"Who? Do you know?"

"I know a couple of them. Mark Hanson, Henry Michael, and Kyle Benton. They used to rodeo together."

"Do they know that you inherited the ranch?"

"I don't think so. I told everyone my parents sold the ranch to pay off some debts."

"You said Hank wanted this place bad?"

"Yes, but what of it? He thought this place had gold on it and that was why he wanted it so badly. When we were dating I told him the story of Golden Meadow and old Henry Singer and his mule Goldie."

"Logan told me that story and how no one ever found his mineshaft lined with gold. Do you think there's any truth to the story?"

"I don't know. Like any folklore, it probably started from something. But a shaft lined with gold? I have my doubts."

"You know, I found an old mineshaft about six years ago fixing fence. I didn't think anything of it; in fact I built a fence across the front of it so the cattle wouldn't wander in. Logan said he didn't remember ever seeing that one before, and we joked at the time about it being Old Henry's."

"Did you ever go into it and see where it went?"

"No, we were pretty busy, and I'm not much of a fan of underground holes."

"Justin, I have to go make a phone call, I'll be right back." She was out of bed, dressed, and down the stairs before he could ask any more questions.

"If someone is trying to frame this Love cult, I think they would like to know it," Jesse said to herself as she picked up the receiver and dialed information.

"Hello. I would like the phone number for Mayor Teller Love."

"Hold one moment, please, I will connect you," the voice replied on the other end of the line.

"Hello, this is Mayor Love, what can I do for you?" Jesse didn't recognize the man's voice, so that was a good thing. She knew they were still bad people so she didn't want to give up too much information. But she thought if she could stir them up enough to want to try to figure this out, it would be beneficial to her.

"Hi, sir, my name is Jessica Walker, you don't know me. I am recently back home in Danville and I wanted to talk to you about a problem I'm having."

"It's nice to meet you, Jessica. What is it I can do for you?"

"Someone has been killing my cattle. They even killed my friend's dog and my horse. I have been shot at and had a good friend killed and placed in a sack. They left us two notes and signed their name 'Love.'"

"You don't think I had anything to do with it, do you?"

"I know your group's story about Arizona and California. I know all about your plight and this doesn't fit your M.O. So, no, I don't think it is you, but I do think someone is trying to set you up."

"You said you know about us. How?"

"A lot of research, but that isn't the problem. I want these people punished for what they're doing to me and for setting you up."

"I'm listening, but I think we had better meet and talk this over and try to figure out who it is. Where do you want to meet me?"

"Do you know where the Running W Ranch is in Danville?"

"Yes."

"Why don't you come for dinner at six tonight. We can talk then."

"Sounds good, I will see you then. And Jessica, I promise I will try to help in any way."

"Thank you."

As she hung up the phone, she heard Justin enter the kitchen.

"Who was that, Jess?"

"Mayor Teller Love. He is going to help us."

"You called a Love? Why? I thought they were the enemy."

"They are, but I think there is someone else as well, and if the mayor thinks that we trust him then he may help us find the other person involved."

"I see." He really didn't, but he figured he would let this idea run. It was the best one so far.

"I invited him to dinner at six."

"Do you think that's the best idea?"

"I don't know what else to do. We have to push his hand a little to get something to use on him."

"I hope you know what you're doing. These people are dangerous."

"I know, but how else are we going to make them nervous if we don't make them think we are calling in the FBI to investigate?"

"That's not a bad idea. We can tell him we have already contacted them and that they will be here within the week to do a full investigation on the matter."

"Maybe he will be so worried that he sends his people out of town until this whole thing blows over. Then if the killings stop we know it was his group."

"And if they don't?"

"Then we know we have someone else who wants us to suffer."

"Jess, I'm starving. Can we get some breakfast?"

"Yes, I guess you earned some. What do you want?"

"French toast, bacon, and eggs."

"Good thing you aren't too demanding."

Jesse got some coffee going and cooked Justin's breakfast to order. They sat and talked about what they would say to Mayor Love until the food was gone and the coffee pot was on its second fill.

"Good breakfast, Jess, you can cook for me anytime."

"Well thank you for that privilege."

"What do you want to do first today?"

"Feed my horses."

"Too late for that."

"What do you mean?"

"I fed them before I came to see you about the letter. I wanted to make sure nothing else was harmed last night."

"Thank you for that."

"I had better call Grandpa and Grandma and let them know I'll be helping you today."

"Yes, and I should see how Marnie is doing."

Justin quickly dialed Logan and Mary's place, and after a few rings Mary picked up. Jesse listened as they conversed and told about their plans for the day.

"How is Marnie doing, Grandma?"

"The poor woman has been up almost the whole night searching through that laptop of hers for answers."

"Well, she has been a huge help," Justin said before he hung up the phone.

"Let's go to town. I need to see Bill." Jesse grabbed her sweater and headed out the door, Justin close on her heels.

Out in the driveway they saw Marnie coming towards them. She looked like she had a lot of thoughts running through her mind. They watched as she fumbled through the papers in her arms and mumbled to herself.

"Marnie, what's up?" Jesse asked as they approached her.

"Jess, I think I figured it out!"

Chapter 18

Jesse couldn't believe it! "You what? How? Who is it?" Marnie had never struck her as an investigator.

"Hank."

"Hank? How could it be? I called him this morning."

"What time?"

"Four or five o'clock. But I called Caldwell and he was home."

"Impossible, Jess. I got his phone records. All his calls have been automatically forwarded to his cell phone in Republic."

"What? You mean he's in Republic?"

"Well, if he isn't, according to phone records his cell phone is. A friend got the information for me."

"What friend do you know who could get that kind of information for you?"

"Oh, once I slept with a guy named Rolando Roquemore. He worked for Mexican bigwigs of some kind and he said if I ever needed anything to call him. So I did."

"Marnie, you and I have got to sit down and talk about your past someday. You haven't told me everything about those days you spent out of Caldwell."

"And, Jess dear, I may never tell you either." Marnie wasn't a very secretive person and her story wasn't a very interesting one to say the least. At one time, she worked as an intern for the Department of Revenue and got to meet a lot of powerful people.

"What do we do? He may already know I'm here and I have the ranch. What if he files for half the ranch in the divorce and they find out I have been hiding it from him? I could be in a lot of trouble. He could get half of it."

"Calm down, Jess. I have never seen you like this before. He committed adultery so he's not entitled to anything in the divorce. They can trace it if they go back through your paperwork, but otherwise everybody says that Mary and Logan bought the ranch."

"I know. I just panicked, that's all."

Justin put a reassuring arm around her shoulders and pulled her close to him. To both their surprise, she didn't pull out of his embrace in front of Marnie. Jesse guessed she had found a comfortable place in Justin's arms and didn't want to move. Instead, she drew even closer.

"Mary and I are going to take her van and go to Republic and see if we can find or get a glimpse of Hank anywhere there."

"Good idea. Justin and I are going to Golden Meadow to see if we can find any clues as to who shot at us up there."

"Be careful." With that said Marnie gave Jesse a hug and then she turned back towards Mary and Logan's to set her plan for the day into action.

Jesse hated to move away from Justin but she knew they were never going to get to Golden Meadow and back for dinner with Mayor Love if they didn't get going.

As they entered the barn, Jesse was happily surprised to see a beautiful buckskin gelding in Cozy's old stall. The pain of what happened there just a couple of nights before was so fresh she swore she could still see bloodstains in the straw. However, she knew that was foolish since Logan had cleaned the stall and disinfected it thoroughly.

"That's Monty. Monty, this is Jesse, be nice to her."

Jesse smiled at Justin's introduction to the horse. She looked him over and liked what she saw. She could tell at a glance he was a product of good breeding.

When she opened the door, he quickly came over to meet her and nudge her hand with his nose.

"Hi, Monty, how are you?" The horse licked her cheek as she scattered kisses along his muzzle. "You're a sweet boy, aren't you?"

"Will he do for you, Jess?" He watched in delight as Jesse and Monty made instant friends. He knew how Monty felt. He was fond of Jesse too, and after this morning, he wasn't sure he could ever let her out of his sight again. He felt a tinge of jealousy as he watched Jesse kiss the gelding.

"He's wonderful. I will take good care of him for you." Justin smiled and went to get Badger out of his stall and saddle him.

After he had gotten Badger saddled, he stopped back by where he had left Monty and Jesse and was surprised to find Monty saddled and in his stall with Jesse still kissing and cooing to him.

"Hey, if I would have known he was going to get all of your affection I would have left him out in pasture."

"Are you jealous?" Jesse asked, turning to lead Monty out of the stall.

"As a matter of fact, yes I am."

Jesse walked up to Justin and smiled up into his blue eyes.

"What are you going to do about it?"

"I'm going to turn him back out to pasture."

"The hell you are!" Jesse wrapped both arms around Justin's neck and smiled as she pressed her lips against his nose.

"Happy now? I kissed your nose too."

"I'm not happy yet." Justin smiled as he pressed his lips to hers and felt her melt against him. After a few moments Jesse broke the kiss and went to turn around. Justin caught her waist and pulled her against him.

"Wait a minute. How many kisses did you give that horse?"

"Lots. Why?"

"I expect twice as many tonight as he got."

"You do, huh? We'll see if you're as good as he is today," Jesse teased.

"Better, and you know that already." Justin kissed her again in a promising way. Jesse shivered against him.

"You had better watch it or I will make you prove that to-night."

"Gladly, anytime. In fact I have half an hour if you'd like to see now." Jesse's face flushed.

"We had better go find bad guys."

"Yes, I guess you're right. Shall we take a rain check?" Justin scattered kisses along her neck and collarbone.

"What am I going to do with you?" Jesse smiled as she leaned up and brushed a soft kiss across Justin's lips.

"Anything you want, and I'm afraid you know that."

An hour later they were riding towards Golden Meadow. Jesse followed Justin closely, keeping a wary eye for anything amiss among the trees and mountains that made them an easy target.

Jesse's mind wandered to the idea that Hank could be out there somewhere looking for her and seeking revenge for divorcing him. She hadn't heard any word yet from her lawyer, but she couldn't imagine Hank caring that much whether he had her or not. At least not enough to want her dead.

When she had seen him in bed with that woman he never even made the effort to go after her or say anything that would make her want to stay. He just rolled over and most likely continued with what he was doing after she left.

Everything seemed to be pointing towards him as the culprit. Behind all of this was the discovery of his cell phone records going to Republic. That was a huge thing. Nevertheless, she knew that was him who had answered, and he didn't sound like he was hiding anything.

It just didn't make sense to her. Any of it: killing Jack, the cattle, or Cozy. Hank loved Cozy as much as she did, even though he may not have liked her. Cozy had paid a lot of bills barrel racing.

"Justin?" Jesse whispered.

"Yes."

"Where is that cave you said you saw when you were fixing fence?" Jesse had an idea—if it was Hank, maybe he was after gold or something stupid like that.

"Up on the fence line towards Golden Meadow. Why?"

"Take me to it. If you don't mind I have to check something out." With that, Justin reined in and turned his mount to face her head on.

"What are you thinking, Jess?" Jess couldn't tell him everything she was thinking. It wouldn't be at all proper given their circumstances.

"If it's Hank, maybe he knows something we don't. If it isn't Hank, maybe someone is using that cave as a hideout."

After a few moments of hesitation, Justin turned and headed the big gray in the direction of the cave as he remembered. Jesse followed in Justin's wake again and dared not to say a word as they closed in on the spot she guessed must be near the cave.

Justin slowed and pulled his horse to the right into some thick buck brush and dismounted, motioning her to do the same. Jesse dismounted, and using only hand signs she realized they were going to leave their horses there and go on foot so as not to be sitting ducks if her hunch was right.

She retrieved her rifle from its scabbard on her saddle and watched Justin do the same. Simultaneously, they racked a shell into the chambers and again, in Justin's tracks, she followed closely behind.

She watched as he quietly maneuvered around so they could see the front of the cave. Jesse could see a dark hole with a tattered fence in front of it. She knew she had heard Justin right when he said he had built a fence in front of it, but this fence that stood before her looked as though it had been cut.

"I thought you said you had just built a fence not too long ago across there?" Jesse whispered.

"I did. But that's been cut recently." Justin eased forward. He wanted to check for tracks of any kind at the cave entrance.

Jesse stayed in the brush with her rifle aimed at the cave entrance and prepared to open fire should anything occur.

She watched fretfully as Justin closed the gap between him and the cave entrance. He knelt and ran his hands over the dirt. She knew he had found what he wanted.

Justin saw the unmistakable tracks, horse and human, and by the look of the human tracks he was a big man. The dirt at the entrance of the cave was moist, almost muddy, and the tracks sunk down deep.

Justin read the bottom of the track size. A number "13" was clearly readable in the moist dirt. He stood and looked deep into the darkness of the cave; the freshest tracks were coming out.

Right here, in this very cave, a killer stayed. No doubt this was the closest he had ever been to the man who shot at him and was responsible for only God knows what else.

Justin made his way back to where Jesse was hiding, and whispered, "There are tracks. Both horse and rider. What size of shoe does Hank wear?"

"Size ten, I know that for a fact. He weighs one eighty or so." Justin winced. That meant it was someone else, someone much bigger. He guessed the man who made those tracks to weigh close to three hundred pounds.

"How big was that bay gelding you saw in Jack's barn?"

"He was big, maybe fourteen or fifteen hundred pounds, size two shoe, maybe." Jesse winced. What if that was the killer's horse and that guy had seen her come pet his horse that day? "You think that was the killer's horse, don't you?"

"Yes I do. The tracks that are over there in the mud are big tracks, both horse and rider. But I have an idea of how to stop him from killing any more animals or anything else. Let's take a branch and get rid of my tracks at the front of this cave because we want this guy to come back and we don't want him to know we were here."

"We want him to come back? Are you crazy, Justin? We don't want him anywhere close to here ever again."

"Yes we do. We're going to cripple him or maybe even catch him." Justin smiled at his brilliant plan. The cave was dark, and unless the man had a flashlight, which he figured was a 50/50 shot, he would have to start into the cave in the darkness.

"How are we going to do that?" Jesse asked, confused.

"Easy, really. You're going to go back to the ranch and round up any kind of trap you can find—bear, cougar, coyote, whatever. Anything big enough to hold a man."

"What are you going to do?"

"I'm going to hide out and make sure he doesn't come back before we can get this plan set up."

"Isn't that dangerous being out here by yourself?" Jesse didn't want him hurt; she was beginning to really like him. He wasn't selfish or mean and she liked everything about him. She wasn't ready to have him killed.

"I'll be fine. Bring a flashlight and a rope as well. I want to make sure this guy is here when we get back in the morning."

Justin knew they needed to catch this guy, dead or alive. He wanted him alive so he could find out if he was working alone, and if he wasn't, who was helping him with his plan. If he could get a rope around his leg in a snare, he could hang him from a tree for the night.

"I'm guessing from my days in the army I can still draw up a snare. If so, he should be hanging from that big tree in front of the cave when we get back tomorrow morning."

"You're going to hang a man from a tree? That's a little too Marshal Dillon, isn't it?" Jesse laughed to herself. She could picture a man hanging from the tree by his feet and Justin standing below reading him his rights.

"Aren't you the funny one here?" Justin smiled at her attempt at humor. He knew they had to get the plan in action if they were going to get back and have dinner with Mayor Love tonight.

"Okay, I'll be back soon. You be careful."

"You too." With that, Justin pulled Jesse into his arms for a long kiss that ended too soon as far as Jesse was concerned.

She mounted the buckskin and turned back towards the Running W.

It took about half an hour to round up enough traps and get back to Justin at the cave entrance. Justin was eagerly awaiting Jesse's return as she carefully approached the mouth of the cave.

"Over here, Jess," came Justin's soft voice from beside the cave. She turned Monty towards him and dismounted when she approached him. "Did you find enough?"

"I think so. I found four bear traps, one huge trap, and six middle-sized traps."

"Good. I'll take the traps and rope. I want you to go hide your horse down by Badger, grab the flashlight, and follow me."

Jesse did as he requested. After securing her mount, she grabbed the flashlight and headed back towards the mouth of the cave after Justin.

When she found him he was setting traps down in the mud just inside the darkness of the cave. She flipped on the light and held it steady as he set the arrangement of traps.

She watched in wonder as he secured the rope to the largest trap and set it smack dab in the middle of the cave. He then strung the rope out to the tree he earlier pointed out and buried the rope in the mud.

He strung a loop over a large sapling, pulled it tight, and secured it.

"Okay, that should work. Let's get rid of our tracks and go have dinner." They worked together until no sign of them being there was evident to the untrained eye.

"Justin, this contraption you made isn't going to kill this guy, is it?" Jesse couldn't figure out why she cared after what he did to Cozy, her gelding, but she didn't want to be like him and kill someone else. Besides, what if Justin was wrong and this wasn't the killer but just someone who was trespassing?

"It won't kill him. It should just string him up from that tree by his feet. Between you, me, and this mud hole, I'm not one hundred percent sure it's going to work."

"Well, let's get home, we've got a big dinner to get ready for." Jesse was nervous about confronting Mayor Love. What if he had nothing to do with it? What if she was jumping to conclusions? Or, what if he had everything to do with the murders and now was focused on killing her? She knew she was reading too much into this dinner, but she had to watch her back very carefully. For the life of her, she didn't know if she was doing the right thing or not.

Two hours later, Justin and Jesse found themselves pacing back and forth across the kitchen floor watching Mary and Marnie cook dinner.

"Marnie, did you see anything in town today?" Mary asked to take her mind off of Jesse and Justin's pacing.

"No sign of Hank. I went to the hotel where the phone number was last tracked to, but they said a woman now occupied the room. There was a man there who fit the description of Hank about a month ago, but he only stayed two days and then checked out."

"A month ago he was in Billings, at a rodeo," Jesse chimed in.

"They identified him from a group of photos I had as staying there on April 5th."

"I'm telling you, on April 5th he was in Billings. He got bucked off and blackened his right eye," Jesse said.

"What if he lied to you and was really up here?" Marnie said as she stirred the corn.

"He didn't even know I had the ranch, Marnie."

"Maybe she has a point. What if Hank didn't care if you had the ranch or not. You said he believed the story about the gold. Secretly, he may have been coming up here searching for gold instead of going to rodeos," Justin added as he paced back and forth.

"That would make sense. He stayed in a drunken state after I told him my parents sold the ranch to Logan and Mary for a past debt. He was so determined to get it back any way possible."

"Call his phone number again," Justin said. "See if he answers. Ask him how he's doing and where he is."

"Okay," Jesse said. She walked to the phone and dialed his phone number as she paced the floor. It rang three times and went straight to his voicemail. Jesse hung up the phone.

"All I'm getting is his voicemail."

"For the love of Pete! Will you two let us finish dinner? Stop pacing and go check horses or cows or something," Mary exclaimed as she waved a spoon in front of their faces and placed it back in a vat of mashed potatoes.

"Sorry, Grandma, I guess I didn't realize we were bothering you two."

Logan stepped in from the porch and smiled a weak smile at Jesse and Justin, who had taken a seat at the table.

"Well, what did you two find out up on the range today?"

"Well, we found a cave and fresh human and horse tracks," Jesse replied.

"Really? Do you think it was them?"

"Yes we do," Justin answered.

"No, we do not. Oh my gosh, I have to go to town real quick!" Jesse exclaimed.

"What? Jesse, Mayor Love will be here any moment. What are you talking about?" Marnie asked.

"I have to go talk to Bill. Marnie, you and Justin know as much if not more about this whole cult thing than I do. Just find out anything you can. I will be back as soon as I can."

"You're crazy! You can't head to town alone." Justin knew he shouldn't tell her what she could or couldn't do, but he was worried about her.

"Do you think Bill has something to do with all this?" Logan asked.

"No, not at all, but I think he has an idea who does. Justin, remember when I told you he was acting real weird the other day? Well I think someone was in the store he could point us towards."

"Jess, just be careful," Justin asked as he stood next to her while she put on her jacket and headed out the door. He followed her outside to her truck.

"I will be fine. I promise. I'll be careful."

"You'd better, because if you die, I'm giving Monty to Karla." Justin knew that would get her hackles up and make her make sure to get back to him.

"You wouldn't dare." She leaned close and kissed him solidly on the mouth. He kissed her hard back.

"For whatever it's worth, Justin, I care a lot about you and I want you to know that, whatever happens and even though you don't believe in love. I love you and every little flaw you have." Jesse knew she shouldn't tell him, but she didn't know what the night would bring and she wanted to make sure he knew how she felt.

"Wow! You sure know how to throw a wrench into a man's plans." Justin somehow wished he had said it first, but she had beaten him to it. He had sworn off good women, but Jesse was a good woman with a lot of love to give and she owned the ranch he worked for so she couldn't be after him for money.

"What are you talking about, Justin?"

"I told you—"

Jesse clamped her hand over his mouth and cut him off.

"Justin, it's okay if you don't love me. I told you that before anything happened. I understand. I just wanted you to know how I felt, nothing more. I didn't expect it in return."

Jesse knew she was lying to herself, as she wanted him to love her back as much or more than she loved him, but she knew it wasn't going to happen. She was determined to live with it until she could make him see the error of his ways and know that he couldn't live without her.

"You know, if you would stop cutting me off when I'm talking I could say what I was going to say."

"Sorry." Jesse saw Logan come out onto the porch and motion for Justin to come in. "I'd better go. We can talk about this later."

"See you later, Jess." Justin ran across the driveway to where Logan was standing. Jesse started her truck and headed for town. She was thinking about everything that had happened in the past few days and had a lot to take in. She wasn't sure when everything clicked, but it did, and she thought maybe she had it figured out in some strange way.

"Jesse, wait!" Justin yelled as he darted down the driveway behind her. Jesse looked in the rearview mirror and smiled as she saw Justin race after her. She jumped out and hurried to meet him.

"What's wrong?"

"Mayor Love called. He couldn't make it, so I am going to town with you. Besides, you owe me an explanation for this whole trip. I'm not sure what you're thinking."

"Jump in, I will see if I can explain it to you so you will understand."

Once they were on their way to town, and after a few sidelong glances from Justin, Jesse began the best she could.

"Okay. About three years ago, Hank and I were in Denver at a rodeo. While we were behind the chutes, he punched me. At the time I thought it was for something else, or maybe even an accident, but now it makes sense in a strange way. I heard him talking to a man named Laser Love about gold. At the time I thought they were talking about winning bull riding. You know, winning the gold buckle and all that macho junk. But now after all these killings, and other stuff that has been happening for the past three years, I may have put two and two together."

"Yes, you're right. I'm following you, but where is this heading?"

"I told you Hank always believed there was gold on this place, and he went on a drunken spree when he learned my parents had sold it. He wanted us to buy it back."

"So you think he's been trying to scare the new owners off all this time? But with his cell phone being in Republic, the note, Jack, and Cozy, you think he knows you're here."

"Yes I do. But I think he has help, a big man with a big bay horse."

"So where does Bill come into all of this?"

"Someone was in that shop that day, someone he didn't want to know that he knew me. What if it was Hank's helper? He would be able to identify him and point us in the right direction. We could sit outside their place and wait for Hank to show up."

"So you don't think the Loves have anything to do with this?"

"I think they are a very clever cover-up. Oh, I think they're guilty of kidnapping and drug smuggling, but I don't think they're murderers."

They turned down Main Street and pulled up in front of the saddle shop. The lights were on and the sign said open. They quickly made their way inside.

"Bill!" Jesse yelled. No reply came from behind the curtains.

"Maybe he went to the store or something?"

"I don't think so, he wouldn't leave his shop open. I'll go check in his office."

"I'll go outside and look on the street in case he grabbed a bite to eat or something."

"Good idea." She watched as he made his way outside. Then she walked towards the back office. As she pulled the curtain aside she realized something wasn't right. A half hide of leather lay in a water bath. She felt the water—it was cold, and a wave of dread came over her. Bill had always taught her never to leave leather in water longer than a few minutes, and always warm water.

Jesse didn't want to find another dead body waiting for her in Bill's office. So she turned and ran outside to Justin and relayed what she had found.

"I'll go check in his office. You stay here."

Justin winced as he entered Bill's office and found him behind the desk with an awl hammered into his skull. A quick feel of his hand revealed he had been dead for many hours. Justin found a jacket on the chair and covered him with it.

"We'll find them, Bill, I promise." Justin hadn't realized Jesse had entered the room until she screamed. A glance brought his attention to what she had screamed at.

As Jesse entered the room she had prepared herself to find Bill murdered. She knew deep down he wasn't alive, but she hadn't prepared herself to find a message to her written on the wall in Bill's blood.

Dear Jesse,
I warned you two to stop screwing around. Hope you enjoyed it as much as I'll enjoy killing you!

"How could anyone know what we did?" Jesse asked as she fought back tears that were threatening to fall.

"I don't know, but why wouldn't he threaten to kill me instead of you, Jess?"

"Because I lied to him about the ranch and I filed for a divorce."

"But he cheated on you with another woman."

"That's not how he looks at it. I lied and I left him. I don't even deserve to live." Jesse knew she was being ridiculous. How could the man she had loved for ten years be the same man who now wanted her dead? However, there were no other clues that pointed to anyone else.

"What do we do?"

"Call the police and report this. But first help me clean up this wall. If the police see this message they'll know I have something to do with it, and after the letter at your house they will know we slept together."

"It's illegal to alter a crime scene."

Jesse knew that. She didn't know what else she could do. Maybe pack up everything she owned and move to somewhere Hank couldn't find her. Unfortunately, she knew that place didn't exist.

"I don't know what else to do, Justin."

"Then you go get some rags. I'll get a bucket of soapy water and we will see what we can get done."

They set about their task of cleaning the message off the wall. Once that was accomplished, they knew they had one more phone call to make to the police, hopefully their last one of this nature.

It didn't take long for the police to get there and go about their normal routine of asking stupid questions and fudging up the crime scene.

Chapter 19

The next morning the sound of rain pounding off the roof woke Jesse. She glanced at the alarm clock—it showed six thirty.

She stretched and smiled when she realized she wasn't alone in bed. Justin lay sound asleep next to her. She couldn't believe she had a reason to smile after all that had happened. After finding Bill, the message, and dealing with the police the night before, it was well after ten o'clock when they had returned from town.

It seemed like second nature waking up next to him even though she had only spent a morning and one full night next to him in slumber.

She knew she had found her missing piece and her puzzle was almost completed. Now if only they could solve all these murders and settle down and be normal people.

Jesse climbed out of bed and dressed quickly. It was almost light outside and she wanted to get up and check on Justin's traps.

After a quick cup of coffee, she went out and fed Boe and the other horses in the barn. She stopped and looked in on Monty as he ate his grain. He was a beautiful gelding. He sensed her watching him, came up to the door, and nuzzled her cheek.

"Good morning to you, beautiful."

"I thought that was my line," Justin said as he came up behind her and hugged her.

"Good morning to you too." Jesse smiled.

"You leave me for a kiss from a horse?" Justin smiled as he turned her around to face him.

"Yes, well, he is definitely less trouble than you."

"Yeah, I bet he is." With that, Justin kissed her softly. "But can he do that?"

"Not quite as good, but close." Jesse smiled and leaned against Justin's shoulder.

"So what does our day look like?" Justin asked.

"Wet," Jesse admitted.

"Wow, good observation. I knew I brought you along for something."

"Wait a minute, you brought me along? More like I brought you, mister."

"So what are we doing today?"

"Well, I thought we would go check on your traps first."

"I'll get the horses saddled if you want to throw some food together." Justin hated to part from Jesse but he knew the day had to get going at some time.

"Sounds fair. I think we should take a rifle or two along as well. Don't you?" Jesse had been thinking about what would happen if someone were hanging upside down in that tree. She knew they wouldn't be very happy with them and they most likely would have a gun handy.

"I think that's a good idea. I'll meet you out here in half an hour." They each went about their tasks. Jesse got some food together, two rifles, and enough shells to win World War III.

She also threw in a couple of flashlights, just in case, and quickly wrote a note for Marnie letting her know where they were. She also decided to put in the note that if they didn't see Justin and her by nightfall, to call the police and send them up after them. She left directions to the cave that even a blind man could follow.

The ride up was slow and cautious. Jesse feared what they would find, but feared worse that they may find Hank hanging upside down from that tree.

She knew he had something to do with it, but she couldn't imagine this being run or devised by him. Hank was just a stupid bull rider. It wasn't like he was a rocket scientist or something. Hell, he hadn't even graduated high school.

As they neared the cave, Jesse's heart leaped into her stomach, for she could see fresh tracks in the mud, even with the rain. She knew Justin saw them, for he reached behind him and grabbed his rifle from its scabbard.

They heard a whinny up ahead and gasped as a big bay came running towards them. Justin was out of his saddle and pulling Jesse down with him before they could tell it had no rider aboard.

"Maybe you caught him?" Jesse whispered as they both realized the rider had to be at the cave.

"Maybe not." Justin helped her up and pointed for her to hide the horses over the bank. She did as directed, even taking the big bay with her. When she was finished tying them up, she crawled back up so that she could watch Justin as he circled around to the top of the cave.

Justin could see the top of his rope but couldn't see the bottom yet to see if someone was caught. He maneuvered higher until at last he could see what he wanted to see—two feet caught in his rope dangling from the tree.

"Thank God," Justin sighed in relief. He knew that the shooter was caught.

He plunged down off the hill and came up behind the dangling man.

"Don't move, mister! I have a gun aimed directly at your head!" he ordered. The man didn't move. Justin moved closer and cringed as he realized the man's lifeblood was in a puddle on the ground below him.

Jesse was at his side in minutes with her rifle in hand.

"What's wrong, Justin? Who is he?"

"I don't know yet."

"He's dead, isn't he?" Jesse knew from the size of the man it wasn't Hank.

"Yes, he must have hit his head on the tree as it flung him up," Justin figured aloud. That wasn't how he had wanted it.

"Who is he?" Jesse asked.

"I don't know, I haven't seen his face yet." The large man hung before them with his back to them and his jacket hanging over his face, his identity a secret even in death.

"That's the bay horse that was at Jack's place, so I know whoever he is, he's Jack's killer." For that reason Jesse knew what they had done wasn't in vain.

She watched as Justin swung the big man's carcass around so they could see his face. Justin lifted the hem of the jacket to reveal the killer's face.

Jesse looked deep into the face of the ugly man whose beard and mangy hair covered most his face. She didn't know him at all.

"Justin, I have never seen him before in my life," Jesse admitted.

"No, you wouldn't have." But he had; he had seen him a lot in his life. A look of confusion was all Jesse could recognize as she looked at Justin.

"His name is Charlie Firestone, but I have no clue why he's here," Justin admitted in a shallow voice that Jesse didn't recognize.

"How do you know him?" Jesse asked.

"He was Annie's brother." Justin grimaced. Maybe it wasn't Jesse they were after. Maybe it had been him, but that didn't make sense either, and now his only witness couldn't talk.

"You mean your ex-girlfriend? But what would her brother be doing up here?" Jesse was confused. She had never known Annie or his brother. Why would they be after her?

"I don't know what he would be doing up here, but that's him." Justin had never liked Annie's brother Charlie. He had always been a creepy man. Annie had never seemed to care for him much either, or so she had said.

He wondered how she would take his death and the fact that it was Justin who brought him to it.

"Why would he want Jack dead?" Jesse couldn't figure it out. Her mind swirled with whys and hows. Nothing was making sense. If it had been Hank hanging there, it would have made more sense to her.

"Did he hate you for breaking up with his sister?" It was all she could come up with. Maybe it was revenge for his sister's broken heart.

"There was never any love lost between us, but I don't think he would kill these people and animals because of Annie and I breaking up."

"Do you think this was just a coincidence that he was Annie's brother and maybe Hank hired him to carry out his evil plan?"

"I think that may be a little closer to the truth, Jess." Justin still stared into the unseeing gaze of Charlie Firestone's face. There were a lot of unanswered questions that he needed the answers to.

"I'll be right back." Jesse turned and went back to where the horses were tied and retrieved the flashlights.

"What are those for?" Justin asked as Jesse joined him once more in front of the cave.

"I want to know what's inside this cave." Jesse had to know why everyone was dying. Who knows, maybe they had found some gold.

"I'll lead the way, just watch out for the traps we sunk in the mud." Justin flipped on his light and headed into the darkness of the cave. Jesse cautiously followed in his exact footsteps.

The two lights did precious little against the darkness of the cave. They made their way almost two hundred yards into the cave with no sign of anything but footprints and horse tracks.

"Justin, look up towards the roof of the cave." Jesse had been catching something shiny every now and then shining back at her from her flashlight beam. She was surprised when she focused closer on what it was. It looked like a lantern.

"I see it." Justin reached up and lit the wick with a match from his pocket. The light quenched the darkness for about fifty feet.

"This shines better than these flashlights." Justin started forward again, this time with the lantern as his light.

"How far have we gone?" Jesse asked.

"I'm guessing about two hundred yards or so."

"How far do you think this goes in?" Jesse asked.

"No idea." They walked in silence for a long time. Jesse looked at the walls of the cave for any sign of gold or any other ore that might make someone want to kill to get this land.

After a few minutes Justin stopped and looked ahead, confused. "What's wrong, Justin?"

"The cave splits into two different directions. Which way do you want to go?"

"Which way is Golden Meadow from here?"

"I would guess we go to the right, that's the way the tracks go."

"Then let's go that way." Jesse knew that if this was the old miner's cave it had to come out somewhere by Golden Meadow.

They walked another two hundred yards or more before Justin stopped abruptly.

"It looks like the cave opens up wider ahead. Maybe this was where Charlie lived or stayed."

They cautiously moved forward until they were standing in the middle of the large underground opening. Caverns ran off on every side of them into the darkness, a large fire pit stood in the center of the opening, and lanterns lined the walls on either side. A small gate they could see was across one tunnel, so they guessed it must have dead-ended and Charlie must have used that tunnel for a horse pen for the big bay.

"Oh my gosh, there must be twenty different tunnels. How do we know which one to take?" Jesse exclaimed.

"We don't. We will just have to start ruling tunnels out one at a time. But first let's light these lanterns, so we have lots of light."

With the lanterns lit, they started exploring the different tunnels. They soon found many of them were dead ends. They had explored about half when they decided to look for footprints and see which one was the most traveled. They found two tunnels that looked well used. One headed from what they guessed was north and the other east towards Golden Meadow.

"I would bet you that the north one is a dead end. Let's check that one out first." Justin said as he motioned to the tunnel.

"That's a good plan." They had barely entered the north tunnel. Jesse was holding Justin's hand when she felt him tense beside her.

"What's wrong?" Jesse asked.

"I smell something." Jesse had smelled it too, but she had just chalked it up to mold and mildew from the wet caves.

"What is it?" Jesse asked.

"It smells dead, whatever it is." Justin was worried and felt the hair on the back of his neck stand straight up.

"I don't want to find any more dead bodies, Justin." She had had enough dead bodies and bloody bags to last her a lifetime. If she never saw another dead animal it would suit her just fine.

"Maybe you had better let me go first." Justin eased ahead of her down the tunnel. They had gone scarcely a hundred yards when they saw the remains of a body dumped in the tunnel ahead of them.

"That's a body up there!" Jesse's voice quaked with fear of who it was this time.

"I see it, Jess. Let's go see if we know who it is." They moved slowly up to it. The smell was so bad that they had to pull their shirts over their noses. As they got closer, Justin saw Jesse start to turn white.

The body lay on its side with its face away from them. Justin reached down and rolled it over. The face of a man came into view, a bullet hole between his eyes.

"Oh my gosh!" Jesse screamed as she turned and ran back down the tunnel as fast as she could. Justin was on her heels. He caught hold of her as they came into the light of the wide spot of the cavern. She flung herself into his open arms.

"Do you know who that was?" Justin asked.

"Yes, it was Hank." Jesse couldn't believe he was dead. She didn't love him. She may have loved him when they were younger but not anymore, but she hadn't wanted him dead either. He deserved to die if he was behind all of the murders and the death of Cozy but she hadn't wanted him shot between the eyes and dumped in an old cave to rot like a discarded dog no one wanted.

"Jesse, I have one small problem that I am having a big problem with," Justin confessed.

"What's that?"

"If that's Hank and he's been dead long enough to start stinking, he couldn't have killed Bill yesterday."

Jesse hadn't thought of that, but now that Justin said it she realized he was right.

"So if he didn't kill Bill, then who did?"

Justin never got the chance to answer. The sound of a gunshot and Jesse's body crumpling before him sent a whole new batch of fears into his mind. His mind raced as he searched the walls for the shooter, with no luck.

Jesse felt the lead rip through her shoulder and cried out in horror as the pain racked her body. She fell to the damp cavern floor.

"Justin, I've been shot." Justin was down by her side and quickly patching the wound on her shoulder when another shot ripped through her left thigh. Justin watched in horror as Jesse fought for consciousness.

"Stop it! Whoever you are, shoot me, not her!" Justin yelled as he grabbed the rifle and shot towards where the bullets had come.

Quickly he picked up Jesse and headed towards the east tunnel. Once he was safely inside, he set Jesse down and quickly checked her wounds in the darkness. Her wounds were bleeding badly but they had missed all vitals as far as he could tell. He had to get her out of these tunnels or she would join Hank in death.

He quickly ripped his shirt into lengths and shoved it into the holes in her shoulder and leg to stop the bleeding.

"Please don't die, Jesse! I don't know what I would do without you." He knew if there was a way out this tunnel was going to be it, so he picked Jesse up and headed quickly down the tunnel.

Behind him he could hear a muffled voice and the ricochet of bullets off the cave walls. He ran faster down the narrowing tunnel. He had a horrible feeling he had taken the wrong tunnel as it got even narrower and the ceiling lowered a considerable amount. Soon he was on his hands and knees pulling Jesse along with him. He knew they were trapped. When he saw the end of the tunnel, his heart sank.

He moved over the top of Jesse and pushed her as far back behind him as he could, hoping to deflect all the bullets himself. He could hear footsteps coming closer in the darkened tunnel. He lowered his mouth to Jesse's for what he figured was their last kiss.

"For what it's worth, Jess, I love you." Suddenly Jesse moved a little below him.

"I love you too, Justin." Jesse was dreadfully cold; Justin could feel it as he placed a hand on her cheek. In the dark he couldn't see her face at all. But he could hear her breathing and that served as comfort enough that she was alive.

"Where are we?" Jesse stuttered through chattering teeth. Justin knew she was losing a lot of blood. He had to get her to a hospital and quick.

"We're at the back of the east tunnel. We can't go any further. I'm sorry."

"What about the light?"

Justin had heard of dying people seeing lights, but he had always heard they weren't supposed to go to it.

"What light, Jess?" Justin asked with a whisper.

"The one above our heads."

Justin looked up and could almost swear he saw a small crack of sunlight. Quickly he pulled Jesse out of the way and started digging at the ceiling.

Amazingly, he found the dirt soft, and it fell away easily as he dug. The sunlight was getting brighter and brighter as he progressed.

"Jesse, it's working! We're digging ourselves out," Justin whispered a little louder.

Justin spoke as if comforting a child from a dark night. He knew that whoever was behind was getting closer so he had to dig fast. The hole was soon big enough for Justin to ease Jesse through and then himself. To his surprise, he was standing behind the cabin in Golden Meadow.

"It was his mineshaft, Jesse, it was old man Singer's mineshaft."

"Hank was right. Justin, we have to hide and wait until whoever is after us pokes their head up, shoot them, and then it's over for good."

"We can't wait around or you'll die, Jesse. I have to get you down the mountain and to a doctor."

"How far away are our horses?" Jesse asked, confused about the distance.

"Not that far. But they're in the wrong direction. I'll have to carry you straight over the mountain and down through Cougar Canyon to the house. That way we don't have to worry about being stopped by whoever it is."

"That's four miles back to the house," Jesse said as she was getting her bearings.

"I know, but we can't go back to the horses or whoever is after us might find us or be there waiting for us."

"You go after the horses. Just hide me with one of the rifles over there in that buck brush where we found the dead deer. I may be able to shoot them or at least wound one of them."

"Okay, but if you see there's more than one person don't shoot unless it's necessary."

Justin quickly got her hidden and headed back for the horses. He wasn't sure he had ever run so fast in his life. When he finally came within view of the cave he stopped and listened, but heard no sounds coming from within. He swung around behind the cave and found a palomino and a big black mare tied up to a tree. He quickly untied the mares and shooed them down the mountain.

He found their own horses right where Jesse had tied them. After turning Monty and the big bay loose, he mounted his gray and headed back to where he had left Jesse.

As he moved through the Forest Service gate he heard a shot from the meadow below and then two more shots.

"Jesse!" He sunk his heels into the gray and sent him charging down the hillside at a speed saved only for suicide riders.

Justin saw two bodies sprawled face-down in the meadow and watched as Jesse crawled from where he had hidden her.

"Jesse!" he yelled again. She smiled as she saw him running towards her. As he approached her he jumped from the gray, swooped her up in his arms, and hugged her softly. Then he placed her atop the gray and led the gray towards the sprawled bodies of the bad guys.

"Did you see who they were?" Justin asked.

"No, I didn't. I just shot when they came up out of the hole and headed my way."

"I'm proud of you. Let's see who they are and then get you to a hospital and fast."

As they reached the first body Jesse noted that one man was skinny and had a blond ponytail. He looked a lot like the man she had seen in the shop with Bill but remembered that man had dark brown hair, not blond.

This man didn't look familiar to her at all from where she sat, but she figured once Justin rolled him over she would probably know him.

The other man was a blonde also but his hair was short and he was strongly built.

Justin knelt and slowly rolled the bigger of the two bodies over so they could see who the culprit was.

Jesse gasped, for the man looked exactly like Jack except for a large scar down his right cheek.

"Gus," Jesse said.

"Who?" Justin asked.

"Gus. Jack's brother, Gus, the voice from Cozy's stall that sounded like Jack."

"I wonder who this skinny one is," Justin said as he rolled the other body over. Jesse and Justin both gasped, but for different reasons. Jesse realized the skinny man with the blond ponytail was a woman, and a very beautiful one at that. But she looked painfully familiar to her as well.

"That's the woman who Hank was sleeping with!" Jesse couldn't believe her eyes. He must have told her about the gold and brought her with him to get it.

"Annie!" Justin exclaimed.

"That's your ex-girlfriend?" Jesse asked.

"Yes, but I guess we'll never know why she did this."

"Or how she and Hank got hooked up together. Or how Hank got killed and why."

Justin stepped up behind Jesse on Badger and headed home as fast as he could. Jesse wasn't sure when it was, but sometime during that ride home she lost consciousness. She knew that when she awoke again Justin would be at her side.

Chapter 20

Two hours later Jesse was sedated and in surgery to take out the bullets in her arm and her leg. The doctors were worried she might have lost too much blood.

Logan, Mary, Marnie, and Justin were in the waiting room, anxious about news of any kind on Jesse. The room was comfortable with its big soft couches and overstuffed chairs. Logan stood by the soda vending machine and looked down the hall to where they had taken Jesse.

He didn't know if her parents would forgive him if she died. The fact that they were dead didn't make him believe they weren't watching somehow. Heck, he didn't know if he would forgive himself if she died. He should have never let her come home during all that was going on.

Marnie and Mary sat together on one of the large sofas holding each other's hands and talking amongst themselves. Marnie cried into a white hankie that Logan had lent her when she first found out that Jesse had been shot.

Justin would never forget the screams from Marnie and Mary when they saw Jesse after they returned from the mountain.

Even though the ambulance was immediately called, they all knew she was losing a lot of blood. As Jesse drifted in and out of consciousness she would only say she was cold or that she needed to know how Justin was.

Justin couldn't believe all the deaths that had occurred in the past week. He had called the police while he watched Jesse being loaded into the ambulance. He tried to go with her but they said he wasn't a relative.

The police said they would call when they found out anything. The deputy had reminded Justin to stay in town and close by in case they needed anything from him.

When they got Jesse to Republic and the doctors saw the extent of her injuries they immediately stabilized her and flew her to Spokane, almost three hours away by car. He didn't hesitate to jump in his truck and drive the distance. Neither had Logan and Mary, who were only too eager to make sure Marnie was beside her best friend.

Justin knew the police could probably throw him in jail for leaving the county but he didn't care—he had to be with Jesse no matter what.

"Justin, will you stop pacing or they're going to charge more for Jesse's hospital stay," Mary exclaimed.

"What does his pacing have to do with the price of the hospital stay?" Marnie asked, confused.

"Floor repair." Mary and Marnie laughed unsteadily. Justin wasn't in the mood for jokes; one of his best friends and the only good woman he had ever fallen in love with was knocking on death's door. Pacing seemed to be the only thing he could do under the circumstances.

Marnie could see how much Justin worried about Jesse, and she knew deep down her best friend had finally found the right man for her life. Marnie liked Justin and loved the fact that he truly cared for Jesse as much as she did.

Getting up, Marnie walked over to where Justin stood with his face to the wall. She placed a gentle hand on his back and felt him start.

Justin turned and found Marnie staring up at him, her eyes red and blurry from four hours of crying over Jesse.

"She'll be all right, Marnie. I know she will," Justin lied to console her.

"That's funny. I was coming over to tell you the same thing."

"Thanks."

"Would you like to go for a walk? Just down the hall, maybe."

"Yeah, I guess so."

They had barely walked out of the room before Marnie spoke what Justin realized was most likely the reason for the walk in the first place.

"I don't like to meddle in other people's business."

"I can respect that, Marnie. What is it you want?" Justin asked, fearing the response was going to be to stay away from her friend, as far away as he could get.

"I don't know whether or not she has said it, but Jesse loves you. I can see it in her face and I can see it in yours, too, that you love her." Justin still didn't know quite where this conversation was going.

"Are you going to ask me to stay away from her?" Justin looked straight into Marnie's face.

"Would you do it if I asked?" Marnie held her head up as she asked the question she hoped she already knew the answer to.

"No." Justin looked down the hall towards the room they had taken Jesse to. He hoped and prayed she was going to be all right.

"Good."

Justin turned and stared at Marnie.

"What?"

"Did you really think I would tell you to stay away from Jesse?" Marnie almost laughed at the mere thought of it.

"Actually, yes I did."

"Well, then you are crazy. I wouldn't jeopardize my best friend's happiness for all the gold in the mountains."

"I thought you said you didn't like to meddle in people's business?" Justin had to admit his body was drained physically and emotionally.

"I did…and I don't, but if you love her and she loves you, then why don't you two get married?"

Justin looked at Marnie as if he had just seen her for the first time.

"You know, Jesse told me how sweet and soft-spoken you were. I have yet to see it at all." Justin smiled.

"I'm very quiet when I'm in public. But around Jesse and Logan and Mary, and even you, I feel like I'm among family."

"You are." Justin liked the idea of Jesse and him being a family, but he wasn't sure either one of them was ready for marriage.

A hand on Justin's back interrupted their conversation.

"Excuse me. Are you Justin?" a small lady with wide-brimmed glasses asked. She wore a white coat and black pressed pants. She looked like if Justin sneezed she would flee to cover.

"Yes, I am. Who are you?"

"I'm Hailey Thompson. Mr. Montgomery's attorney."

"Oh. What can I do for you?"

"I was informed that Jessica Walker is in critical condition here in this hospital." Justin looked baffled. What would Hank's attorney want with Jesse?

"She is."

"I was also informed that you know her very well," Hailey went on.

"Yes, I guess you could say that."

"I'll get to the point then. Jesse filed for a divorce and I received word that Hank was killed."

"Yes and yes."

"On the very same day I received word of both."

"But they didn't happen on the same day."

"I know that. But if you are Jesse's friend then you will try to understand the spot I'm sitting in. Hank was my client, Jesse was my friend. God help me if anyone ever finds out I'm doing this."

Justin looked the lady up one side and down the other. He didn't understand where she was going with this. "I'm not following you."

"How is Jesse?" Hailey asked.

"She was shot twice and is now in surgery. We haven't heard anything else yet."

"She'll be fine. She's one tough cookie."

"Yes she is. But I still don't understand how come Hank's attorney is worried about Jesse and her filing for a divorce." Justin stopped and smiled at the little lady who had to be pushing sixty years old. "Unless…"

Hailey smiled broadly and her whole face lit up.

"I think you're figuring it out."

"Hank has a life insurance policy, doesn't he?"

"A big one." Hailey held her arms out wide as a huge gesture to the size of the policy.

"And it's all Jess's if those divorce papers get lost?" Justin smiled at the lady in front of him.

"Now you're getting it."

"Who said cowboys were dumb?" Marnie added.

"So what do you need us to do?" Justin asked quietly.

"Tell no one what I have just told you." Hailey smiled again, this time less noticeably.

"Mum's the word," Marnie reassured her.

"I don't know what you're talking about," Justin added. Hailey smiled and reached into her pocket and came out with a large envelope.

"That's what I hoped for. Jesse called me two days after she got here and told me about everything. That was how I knew where she was. The divorce papers that I was sent didn't have an address on them, so I followed a hunch when I heard about the shooting of a young woman."

"I'll tell her all of this when she's awake," Justin put in.

"Just let her be surprised when the check comes in the mail. Don't tell her anything except that I wish her a speedy recovery." Hailey didn't want Jesse indebted to her in any way, shape, or form.

She had met Jesse right after she and Hank had been married. She could never figure out what a beautiful young woman would want with an old worn-out cowboy, especially Hank. He was mean, cruel, and a cheat.

"Oh, and give her this envelope for me, will you?" She handed Justin the envelope with Jesse's name on it.

"I will. Thank you, Hailey, for everything you're doing for Jesse." Justin held out his hand for her to shake.

"You're very welcome." After a quick handshake, she turned and was gone just as quickly as she had shown up.

"That was odd," Marnie added, looking down the hall in the direction the lady had left.

"Yes, for you or me. But with Jesse, I'm finding that sort of thing normal."

"She is well liked by all." Justin smiled. He knew what Marnie said was the truth. Jesse had a way of getting under one's skin and making you like her.

"You didn't answer my question. Are you going to marry Jesse?"

"No, I didn't answer your question, did I?"

Justin got another chance to ignore her question as they watched the doctor walk out of the room towards them.

"Are you Justin?"

"Yes, is she asking for me?" Justin couldn't believe it.

"Yes she is, but she's in recovery and you're going to have to wait a little while longer to see her," the doctor emphasized.

"How is she? Is she going to be all right?" Justin prodded the doctor for answers.

"Yes, she's fine. She had a close call with all the blood she lost, but after a transfusion she is doing wonderful. We expect a full recovery."

Justin and Marnie hugged briefly and sank down against the wall as the doctor walked away.

"Thank God," Marnie exclaimed.

"You can say that again."

"Thank God," Marnie said again.

"I don't know what I would have done if I would have lost her, Marnie." Justin placed his head in his hands.

"Probably the same thing I would have done."

"What would that have been?" Justin questioned.

"Curl up and die." Marnie knew it was true. Without Jesse, she wouldn't be able to wake up in the morning and go on living. Jesse had always been her guiding light, in a manner of speaking.

"Pretty close." Justin looked at Marnie and realized that Marnie lived through Jesse's experiences.

"Why aren't you married, Marnie?" Justin asked.

"Men scare me." There it was, she said it. Justin smiled at her.

"Why aren't you scared of me? I'm a man."

"Yes, I know you are. But you're with Jesse and that doesn't pose a threat." Marnie had had a few boyfriends in her life and had never been serious with any of them. Her work became more important than developing a relationship.

"So you're only afraid of men who want you?"

"I guess so. But I'm not sure how this conversation got changed to my love life."

"Just curious."

"You still haven't answered my question."

"For being so quiet and shy you sure are persistent," said Justin as Marnie laughed.

"It's the spy in me."

"You're a good spy, Marnie." She knew Justin was changing the topic again so she decided to go another route.

"Jesse said you're loving with half a heart. Is that true? Have you been jaded by another? Is that the reason you don't want to get married?" Justin frowned at the half a heart line.

"Half a heart, huh?"

"It's a metaphor. For a man who won't give all of himself to a woman because of past circumstances," Marnie explained.

"I gave Jesse my heart the second I met her, and didn't even realize it," Justin confessed.

"Tell me all about it...please," Marnie begged. Jesse had told her so little about their relationship so far and Marnie was a sucker for true romance.

"You will probably want me dead afterwards."

"No. Just tell me, I love romantic stories." She knew it had to be romantic. Maybe they knew it was perfect from the start, or maybe not—that would be even better.

"Romantic? I'm not sure it would classify as that." Justin knew once she heard of how he had shot at Jesse, Marnie would think twice about Jesse's happiness with him.

"I'll be the judge of that." Marnie wanted the details.

"I shot at her." Justin hadn't expected it to come out that way, but it did. Marnie looked at him, dumbfounded. He quickly explained the whole story about her lower lip quivering and the brush stinging her cheek, and the horseback ride to the pickup. When he was finished he looked at Marnie. "What do you think? Am I romantic or what?"

"You shot at her? You gave her your heart when you shot at her? You're right, that isn't romantic. I don't see that written in any romance book anytime soon."

Justin couldn't help it—he threw his head back and laughed. Soon Marnie joined in. Mary and Logan started down the hall towards the sound. It felt good to laugh; after all, Jesse was going to be fine. The bad guys were dead and life was going to be okay.

"What in heaven's name is going on?" Mary asked.

"Marnie doesn't think I'm romantic at all." Justin roared again.

"Well, he shot at Jesse." Marnie laughed.

"Logan, I think they might have left one of those laughing gas tanks turned on around here a little too long. These two have lost it," Mary chimed.

"I'm not sure we have ever had it." Marnie laughed.

"Have you two heard how Jesse is?" Justin suddenly stopped laughing and stood up.

"Yes. She's fine, but we have to wait to go see her for a while, so Marnie and I are going shopping." Justin got it all out with one breath.

"We're what?" Marnie gasped.

"We're going shopping." Justin had something he had to get for Jesse, and who better to help him than Marnie?

"What are we shopping for?" Marnie asked.

"Yes, Justin, what are you shopping for?" Mary asked.

"You'll just have to wait and see." With that he held a hand out to Marnie to help her up off the floor and once she was up he ushered her out of the hospital and to his truck.

A half an hour later Marnie and Justin were walking up and down the aisles of a jewelry store. The man behind the counter kept an inquisitive eye on the couple as they wandered around. Justin was looking into every display.

"What are we looking for?" Marnie asked.

"You know exactly what I'm looking for."

Marnie screamed out in pure pleasure.

"An engagement ring!" Marnie screamed as if it was for her instead of Jesse.

The man at the counter overheard; he saw money in his future. Quickly he made his way to the couple.

"May I help you two? I couldn't help but overhear your conversation. Congratulations to you both." The man was a shifty sort, with a stark white shirt and purple tie. His black pants were stiff and, to Justin, looked uncomfortable. His hair was dark and slicked back along his head with some sort of gunk that made Justin want to touch it just to see if it was sticky or hard.

"Oh, it's not us that are getting married, it's him and my best friend," Marnie corrected.

"Oh." The man looked confused.

"I need an engagement ring," Justin said stiffly.

"How much do you want to spend?" the greedy little man asked.

Justin felt a moment of hesitation. This man would have been a good match for Annie.

"We will talk about price after I see what I want."

Marnie smiled and said, "Jesse doesn't care what you spend." Maybe Justin was in financial trouble.

Justin looked at her. Were his thoughts that evident on his face? "I know. It's just that..."

Marnie smiled at Justin's hesitation. "I could help you out if you want."

Justin laughed, figuring Marnie thought he was poor. He watched as the clerk sunk down in stature. Maybe he thought Justin was in over his head and he wasn't going to be making very much off of him after all.

"I mean I know Jess. She would be happy with a gold band." Justin smiled and knew that what Marnie said was true. Jesse would be happy with a simple gold band.

"Marnie, I'm not poor. I have a lot of money." With this said, the clerk came even closer.

"You do?" Marnie asked.

"Yes. But thank you for the offer." Marnie smiled at the idea of offering Justin money when he had a lot of it himself.

"If you have so much money why do you drive that truck?" She pointed outside to the old blue truck in the parking lot.

Justin laughed. "Jesse didn't like my truck either."

"She didn't?"

"No. Well, maybe it is time for a change," Justin said as he looked out the window and across the street at a Ford dealer.

"A new truck?" Marnie asked.

"Sure, why not?"

"You want a ring first, though. Right, sir?" the store clerk asked hopefully.

"Yes, but I don't see what I want." Justin smiled.

"I can make you anything you want."

"Good. I want you to make me a pretty little ring with a D-ring snaffle bit and in the center I want a large diamond." Justin knew a ring like that would make Jesse say yes.

"Perfect," Marnie added.

"I have no clue what that is. Can you draw it for me?" the clerk questioned, and smiled with uncertainty.

After drawing what he wanted and requesting it be ready in two hours, Justin and Marnie left to go look at trucks.

"Justin, how are you going to ask her to marry you?" Marnie asked as Justin was walking around the dealership looking at new trucks.

"I don't know. I guess just ask her." Justin hadn't really thought about it.

"You have to be romantic."

"She's in a hospital bed. How romantic can I be?" Justin asked as he inspected an F-350 in a dark gray color.

"Do you think Jesse would like this truck?" Justin asked.

"Yes I do. You could get her some flowers."

Justin hadn't thought of flowers.

"Yes, I guess I could. Excuse me, ah, sir?" Justin said to a worker close by.

"Yes, sir," the salesman said as he got closer. "What can I do for you?"

"I want this truck," Justin answered.

"Well then, let's do the paperwork." Marnie followed as the salesman led the way for Justin to the dealership offices.

"Okay, Marnie, so is that all I need is flowers?" Justin asked as they were seated inside to finish paperwork.

"No. If you're going to propose, you have to be romantic." The salesman behind the desk looked up and smiled at Justin.

"You could always buy her a truck, too." Marnie laughed.

"No. She doesn't need that. How did you propose to your wife, sir?" Marnie asked the man behind the desk.

"I'm not married."

"Oh." Marnie backed down.

"But if I was, I would have bought her a truck." Marnie frowned and Justin laughed.

"You're more nervous than I am and I'm the one doing the proposing."

Once the papers were finished, Justin drove Marnie back across the street to the jewelry store.

"Can you drive my pickup to the hospital for me?" Justin asked.

"Yes, I think I can drive that thing."

"Don't worry, it's easy."

Marnie followed Justin inside to see the ring. The clerk set a small black box on the counter and smiled as sweat beaded on his upper lip. "I did it."

"Great, let's have a look." Justin opened the box and stared in awe at the tiny band of white gold with a perfect D-ring bit and a perfect-sized diamond in the middle.

"Justin, she's going to love it," Marnie gasped as she looked into the box.

"Well, sir, what do I owe you?" Justin laughed as the man slid the bill face down across the counter.

He picked it up and smiled. "Well, Jesse can't say I didn't spend enough on her." The clerk smiled as Justin handed him his credit card and placed the box inside his coat pocket.

"I hope she says yes," the clerk said as he handed the receipt to Justin.

"She will," Justin replied.

Chapter 21

The hospital room was dark when Marnie and Justin walked in. Logan and Mary were already inside sitting next to Jesse's bed. Jesse smiled as Justin walked in.

"Hey, I thought maybe you two headed home." Jesse was sure that Justin would be there when she woke up in her room. She was shocked and dismayed when he was nowhere to be found and Logan had informed her that Marnie and Justin had gone shopping.

"How're you feeling?" Justin asked as he made quick work of the distance between the door and Jesse's bed.

"I'm sore. How are you?" she asked.

"I'm fine. Why?" Justin asked, worried she might have thought something had happened to him.

"What was so danged important that you had to leave before you even saw Jesse?" Mary asked.

"I'll tell you later." Justin knew this wasn't quite the right time.

"We had to go get something for Jesse," Marnie chimed in. Justin shot her a keep-your-mouth-shut look. Logan, Mary, and Jesse didn't miss the look.

"You got me something?" Jesse sounded excited.

"Like I said, now is not the time for gifts." Justin looked worried.

"What is it, Justin?"

"Later, Jesse." Logan and Mary were getting the picture that they were a fourth and fifth wheel there.

"Well, honey," Logan said as he stood. "Mary and I had better get going. We have to get home and feed the animals and make sure the police don't leave the gate open for the cows or something to that effect. Besides, I think you're in good hands here." Logan smiled at Justin.

"You call him good hands, do you?" Jesse attempted a smile. Justin wanted to kiss her so badly but he was afraid he would hurt her.

"He won't let anything happen to you or he'll have to answer to me," Mary added.

Jesse said her goodbyes to Mary and Logan and turned to Marnie and Justin.

"Okay, you two, what are you up to? What did you have to go shopping for?" Jesse knew they were up to something.

"I bought a new pickup," Justin exclaimed.

"That was what was so important?" asked Jess as Marnie smiled.

"Well, Jesse, you know men."

"Yes, a couple I do. But I also know that you loved your truck, so why the new truck, Justin?"

"I needed a change."

"You aren't going to tell me, are you?" Jesse smiled.

Marnie could see that they needed to be alone and she was starving anyway, so she figured she would take the opportunity to go get some food.

"I'm going to go get some food. I'll see you in a little while." With that, Marnie turned and exited the room without another word.

"Tell me, Justin. I know you're up to something." Jesse loved secrets. But she couldn't imagine what Marnie and Justin might be up to.

"We did get you something but now is not the time for it. But I promise as soon as the time is right you will get to see it."

"See it? Do I hold it, wear it, or ride it?" Jesse questioned.

"Oh, no you don't. I won't tell you or hint at it. But I will tell you I didn't know that a feed store would carry the right one." Justin was trying to throw her off with the feed store bit.

"A feed store? Is it a new bridle?" Justin frowned. That would be perfect—get her a new bridle and tie the ring to it.

"No, now stop it or I will go against my better judgment and kiss you."

"Why is that against your better judgment?"

"Because you're hurt."

"Yes I am. But I'm not dead, so kiss me," Jesse urged.

Justin leaned down and brushed his lips across hers in a soft, sensuous manner. Jesse felt a quiver run down her spine.

Justin stopped the kiss before Jesse wanted it to stop. He realized a nurse might not like it if they were making love right after she had surgery.

"When you get better, I'll finish that kiss," Justin promised.

"In that case, I'll plan a speedy recovery."

"Good, because I don't know how long I can keep my hands off of you looking at you in a bed." Justin smiled as he watched the color return to Jesse's face.

The door burst open as a nurse ran into the room.

"Are you okay?" she asked in a panicked tone.

"Yes, I'm fine. Why?" Jesse asked.

"Your heartbeat elevated rapidly. We were worried about you. Is he bothering you?" the big-chested nurse asked.

"No, not at all, we were just talking."

"Well, stay off of whatever subject you two were talking about for at least a week," the nurse instructed.

"A week?" Justin barked.

"Yes, and if you were talking about what I think you might have been talking about, she can't do that for a long time," the nurse sternly told him as she left the room.

Justin and Jesse burst out laughing. Justin looked over and saw Jesse watching him.

"Thank you for everything, Justin." Jesse smiled. He had gotten her out of a sticky spot, which she knew she wouldn't have found a way out of on her own.

"You're welcome. And thank you, Jesse." Jesse looked confused. She couldn't imagine why Justin would be thanking her.

"For what?" Justin leaned down and kissed her forehead softly. Then he kissed her squarely on the mouth and smiled as she held her eyes closed, yearning for more kisses.

"For helping me love with a whole heart again." Jesse opened her eyes and looked shocked at what he had said.

"Marnie told you?" Justin shook his head yes. "God, I'm so embarrassed."

"Don't be. You were right."

"So you do love me?" Justin knew this was the perfect spot to give her the ring but he wanted to add it to a new bridle. Marnie had told him to be romantic, so he was going to give it a try.

"So much in fact that I'm going to go and let you get some sleep." Jesse looked upset but she also looked tired.

"I love you, too." Justin watched as she closed her eyes, and soon her breathing was steady and he knew she was fast asleep.

He watched her a few minutes and then turned and exited the room. He had a few things to do before she woke and he wanted to get them crossed off his list.

His first stop was the hospital flower shop. The lady at the counter looked at him strangely when he asked to have all the red and white roses she had delivered to room 293.

"But sir, I have almost three hundred red and white roses in stock. Surely you don't want all of them?" the flower clerk asked.

"I surely do, and I want them delivered while she's sleeping so that when she wakes up they're already there."

"Okay. I can do that. I'll just have to check with the nurse's station first."

"Then do so and hurry up. I have one more thing to get before she wakes up."

"Yes, sir." The lady quickly rang the nurse's station and got approval. "Okay, sir, your wish is our command."

"Great. Oh, and before you ring up the sale I need a gift box," Justin added.

"Okay, we have plenty. Pick your size." Justin did as she instructed and set the box on the counter with his credit card.

"She's a very lucky woman." The lady smiled as she rang up the large order and placed the box in a bright red sack and handed it to Justin.

"No, I'm a lucky man." Justin smiled as he grabbed the sack and headed to the nearest feed store. With any luck they would have what he wanted and he would be back before Jesse woke up or Marnie walked in the room and woke Jesse up.

He also had to stop by a payphone and call the deputy to see what had been taking place back home. He wished all the killings and everything else could just sit on hold until he got Jesse home and healed up. But he knew that wasn't going to happen.

He smiled as he walked down the tack aisles and looked in disbelief at some of the tack that local stores carried. He was so glad that he had gotten Bill to make the stuff for Jesse's store. He didn't have any clue what he was going to do now that Bill was no longer alive.

He picked up a bridle and rolled it over in his hands. "Not too bad. Not exactly what I was looking for, but it may have to do." Justin held it in his hand as he walked down the aisle.

Then he saw it. His eyes settled on it instantly. It was the exact same bridle Jesse had on Cozy. He didn't know if maybe it was too much of a memory for her or not, but he knew she liked it, so he figured it would do.

He grabbed a pair of nice reins and a fancy snaffle bit and curb chain. He looked at the bridle after he put all the components together. It looked good to him.

After making his purchase, he asked to be pointed towards a payphone.

He quickly called the police department and informed them where he was and asked if everything was all right at home.

"We arrested a few of the helpers we tracked down with help from some footprints. We also found a big palomino mare up on the range; we figured she must have been yours. I put her in the barn," the deputy informed him.

Justin knew she was Annie's mare but he wasn't going to say anything to that effect to the police officer.

"Thanks. What about a big bay gelding and a buckskin?"

"I found them and put them in the barn as well."

"Good. Am I in trouble for not being in the county?" Justin asked, fearing but not caring about the response.

"Not really. I knew they moved Jesse to Spokane so I figured I could track you down at the hospital if necessary." The deputy sounded sure of himself.

"That's where I'll be," Justin added for reassurance.

"Good. I will inform you if we find out anything more."

"Thanks. I'll talk to you soon." Justin said goodbye and hung up the phone. He had to get back to the hospital.

In his new truck, he placed the bridle in the box and tied the ring to the browband. Then he replaced the lid and tied the string around the box for safekeeping.

As he stepped off the elevator back at the hospital it was Marnie who was the first he saw.

"Oh, Justin, they're beautiful. I saw them as they brought all the flowers to her room." Justin smiled.

"Good, so they're in the room. Is she still asleep?"

"Yes. The nurses were worried that you wouldn't get here before she was awake. I told them what was going on and they are all on your side." Marnie hadn't been able to help herself. One nurse had asked another within hearing distance what all the flowers were for and she had to answer the question.

"So now if she says no the whole floor will know?" Justin grimaced at the thought of Jesse saying no. He knew she had said that she loved him, but she had also said that she hadn't planned on ever getting married again.

Marnie watched as Justin's face changed from a sure of himself man to a fretful boy in one swoop.

"She'll say yes, Justin. Don't worry."

"I hope you're right." Justin gave her a half-hearted smile, which she returned with a full one.

"I know her. You're just what she wants and needs." Marnie smiled encouragement to Justin, who looked like he might turn around and run at any moment.

"I have only known her a week, Marnie. This is too soon, isn't it?" Justin was getting scared.

"You're perfect for each other," Marnie reassured him.

"She isn't even divorced from Hank yet."

"He's dead. And being married to Hank was a nightmare as far as I hear it. So I think the mourning period is over."

"But he just died yesterday. I'm rushing this," Justin stammered.

Marnie smiled as she watched Justin look for more excuses to run for the hills.

"If she says not right now, then I was wrong and you were right."

"I want yes or nothing. I don't, I mean, I can't be rejected again." Marnie looked confused.

"Again?"

"I thought you knew. I was engaged to the girl that Jesse shot on the mountain. When I gave her the engagement ring she threw it back at me and said I could afford a better one."

The shock of his statement hit Marnie full on.

Everything was starting to make sense now: the moment of hesitation in the jewelry store, the comment about spending enough money on her to make her happy.

"She isn't that girl on the mountain and you know that. She has her own money and she loves you for who you are, not what you have."

"What do you suggest, Marnie?" Justin asked.

"Do you want to know what I would suggest you do? Buck up and go ask the girl to marry you."

"Okay, I'm going to do it." Justin turned and slowly made his way to Jesse's room. Marnie almost laughed out loud. It was like watching a schoolboy ask his first crush out on a date for ice cream, not watching a grown man ask a woman he loved to marry him.

"Good luck," Marnie whispered so that only she could hear.

Justin crept in the door after some pretty odd looks from the nurses and a few encouragements from them as well.

The room was dark. He could hear Jesse's even breathing and knew she was still sleeping soundly. He didn't want to wake her so he sat down in a chair by the bed and waited until she woke up.

He looked around at all the flowers. Maybe he had gone overboard after all. He looked down at the box in his hand that he knew held the answer to the rest of his life's happiness.

If she said yes, they would be married and spend the rest of their lives raising babies and making love.

If she said no, he wouldn't be much worse off than he was, except he probably would quit working for her.

He never remembered it ever being this nerve-racking when he had asked Annie to marry him. In fact he didn't remember being nervous at all. Maybe he should have seen that as a sign.

He looked over to where Jesse was still sound asleep and smiled as he watched her chest rise and fall. He tuned out the monitors and all the subtle noises they made.

He heard a phone ring out at the nurse's station and heard footsteps as someone walked by Jesse's room. The room was comfortable and quiet. The warmth made him wish he could crawl up next to Jesse and fall asleep.

Two hours later he was awoken by Jesse's voice.

"Hey sleepyhead, wake up and come here." Jesse couldn't believe all the flowers in her room when she awoke, or the fact that Justin sat sound asleep in the chair with a large brightly colored box on his lap. She smiled and silently thanked God again for sending him to her.

"Jesse. Oh gosh, I guess I fell asleep." Justin was getting his bearings.

"Is that my gift?" Justin looked down at the box on his lap. Inside he knew was his future, one way or another.

"Yes it is."

"Come over here and let me open it." Jesse loved presents and flowers.

Justin stood and stretched before walking over and sitting on the edge of her bed facing her.

"Here you go, beautiful." He handed the brightly colored box to Jesse.

"Thank you for the roses. How did you know?" Jesse asked as her eyes filled with tears.

"Know what?" Justin hoped they weren't the same kind that had been at her parents' funeral or something like that.

"Red and white roses. They're my favorite." Jesse smiled as Justin lowered his mouth to hers in a slow, meaningful kiss.

"I didn't know that. But they're my favorite, too."

"We have the same taste in flowers," Jesse teased. "Let's see if we have the same taste in whatever else you have for me," she commented as she untied the string and took the lid off of the box.

She suddenly stopped as she eyed the bridle in the box.

It was almost the same one Cozy had. It was perfect, if only she had her own horse to ride again.

"Thank you, it's beautiful, Justin. It's just like Cozy's." Jesse felt her eyes misting over.

"Hey, I thought that might be a good thing." Justin placed a caring hand on her shoulder. He knew she hadn't seen the ring yet.

"It is. It's just that I don't have a gelding of my own to ride with it." Jesse sobbed quietly for Cozy's death yet again.

Justin hadn't wanted her to cry over his gift.

"You can ride Monty until you find a horse you like better." Jesse looked up at this wonderful man who just kept on surprising her.

"I can?" Jesse smiled.

"Of course you can, as long as you take a longer look at that bridle." Justin didn't know how to get her to look closer at it without actually pointing it out.

Jesse rolled the reins over in her hand and looked over the bridle till her eyes hurt.

"It's nice, Justin. Thank you." Justin was getting restless.

"Look again."

Jesse looked confused as she pulled the bridle from the box and turned it over and over in her hands. Justin got up and switched the overhead lights on.

Jesse gasped when the sparkle caught her eye, and she looked closer. At first, it appeared as if the small band of silver was part of the bridle.

"Oh Justin, it's beautiful." Justin realized she hadn't figured it out yet.

"Try it on."

Jesse looked confused again as she looked from the bridle to Justin. "I'm not a horse, Justin."

"I know." Justin laughed out loud. He reached down and untied the ring, and handed it to Jesse. She rolled it over in her hands and took a good long look at the ring.

"Justin," she choked out, "What is this?"

"It's a ring." Justin was now playing with her.

"I know that. But what's it for?" Jesse looked up at Justin through quickly tear-filling eyes.

"Don't cry, Jess. I want you to be my wife." Jesse sobbed as she looked down at the beautiful gold band with a small snaffle bit and large diamond in it.

"Don't say anything yet. I know we haven't known each other very long but I love you with all my heart. I want to grow old with you and raise babies. I want to be with you when my days are numbered. When I die, I want you to be the one holding my hand as I close my eyes for the last time." Justin held his breath while she caught hers and looked at the ring again. "I want to know if you will marry me."

"This is the most beautiful ring I have ever seen." Justin smiled as he watched her toy with her words and hoped she wasn't just trying to figure out a soft way to break his heart.

Jesse knew that Justin had laid everything out on the table and it was now her turn to say yes or no. She deeply wanted to say yes. She had always imagined that if she was ever asked to marry again, she would have the opportunity to jump into the arms of her husband-to-be, not be lying in a hospital bed hoping he would come close enough to grab.

"Justin, I really want to say yes to you. You know how much I love you," Jesse started, and Justin felt the walls close in. This wasn't how he had foreseen this conversation going.

"But?" Justin put in for her.

"But." Jesse stopped and looked around the room at all the roses and then again down at the ring in her hand and the bridle in the box across her lap. She knew what she said now was either going to make or break their relationship.

"If you're going to say no, Jesse, just don't throw the ring. That one is very expensive," Justin ground out through clenched teeth. Justin felt his world crashing down around his head. Quickly a lump formed in this throat.

"I would never dream of throwing this ring at you. It's the most beautiful ring I have ever seen." Jesse still hadn't made up her mind. After all, she was still legally married to a dead man.

"But the answer is no?" Justin replied.

Jesse couldn't look at him. She couldn't figure out if Justin was for her, forever, or if she had to bury Hank first and say goodbye to that relationship before she dove into another.

"You don't have to answer, Jesse. It's okay, I understand. It's too soon. I just thought that if I felt this way about you, you might feel the same way about me." Justin got up. He needed some fresh air.

"Will you stop for a second?" exclaimed Jesse.

Justin stopped but didn't turn to face her.

"I wasn't expecting this. You took me by surprise. I love you so much." Justin turned and looked into her face. "Much more than I ever loved Hank, even in the beginning. I actually love everything about you."

Jesse fumbled her explanation, she knew that, and by the look on Justin's face he still wasn't sure what she was trying to tell him.

"So say yes, Jesse, and marry me," Justin pleaded as he stepped back over to where she lay and lowered his lips to hers in a pleading only their hearts heard and understood.

Jesse's body reacted even though it ached from the holes in it. She moaned as Justin explored her mouth with his tongue.

Justin broke the kiss only after Jesse's heart monitors started beeping. Justin laughed through clenched teeth. He knew no one had ever sent her heart soaring like he did and now she had proof of that. He was the one for her, he knew that, and she was the one for him, if only he could convince her.

The nurse burst open the door and bristled her way past Justin to turn off the beeping noise.

"Well, did she say yes?" the nurse asked as she checked the monitor again.

Jesse smiled at the fact that the nurses knew before her.

"Not yet," Justin replied hastily.

The nurse looked from Justin to Jesse to the ring in her hand and back at Justin.

"You have another ten minutes and then you are going to have to leave," the nurse said as she pushed by Justin again.

"I'm leaving now. Goodbye, Jesse." Justin headed to the door. Jesse looked down at the ring in her hand and slipped it on her ring finger.

"Yes," Jesse whispered.

Justin stopped and wasn't sure his ears weren't playing tricks on him.

"Did you say something?" he asked without turning to look at her.

"I said yes, Justin." He crossed to her again and this time kissed her until the monitors beeped in protest and the nurse came through the door. Once the nurse saw them kissing she knew Jesse had said yes.

"Hey everyone, I think she said yes," the nurse informed the hallway. Jesse and Justin never heard the small round of applause that followed.

"Wow," Jesse said once she broke the kiss.

"Wait until you get better, then I will show you wow." Justin smiled as he watched Jesse flush from his words.

"Jess, I'll see you later. I'd better go before that nurse chases me out of here."

"Before you go, I have a few conditions."

Justin clenched his back teeth as he turned. "What are they?" Justin feared the worst and hoped for the best.

"First, we are going to have a real wedding." Jesse had always wanted a real wedding. She had hated the fact that Hank wanted to elope.

Justin smiled. That was fine by him. She could have whatever she wanted so long as he got her.

"What else?"

"I get to pick the date." Justin smiled again as he moved to sit by her on the bed again. She could plan and arrange this wedding to her pleasure for all he cared. All she had to do was tell him what to say and when to be there.

"Fine. Anything else?"

"One more thing. I want to hire some miners to scout out that cave and look for gold."

"You little gold digger," Justin teased as he kissed her. "You can have all of that and more if you want."

"That will do for now." Jesse laughed.

"You can plan this wedding till it makes you sick of planning. I will do what you want me to and be there when you need me. You can have your gold miners and I hope you strike it rich, because I just did." Justin kissed her again one last time before he got up and walked from the room, leaving Jesse alone with the buzzers and noises of her heart monitor again.

"These nurses are going to hate us before too long." Jesse smiled as she looked down at the small band of gold on her finger.

"Mrs. Justin Wilson." Jesse toyed with the name.

"It'll work."

Chapter 22

Two months later

The sun was bright as it came through the window and warmed Jesse as she lay stretched out on her bed reading the end of the romance book, *To Love With Half A Heart*. Finally, the man in her book found a woman to love forever.

Her life was almost back to normal, and Danville was getting close to being her old hometown again. It seems the murders had caught the eye of a certain young federal agent who she believed had help from Marnie. Now the whole county was crawling with federal agents. They arrested Mayor Love for the kidnapping in Arizona and for three others that could be confirmed he had something to do with.

Thirteen drug busts had taken place while she was in the hospital and many more after she got home. She knew her old hometown was going to be just like it used to be when she was a kid.

She had cabin fever from staying in the house so much recuperating. Mary, Marnie, and Justin called it that. Being lazy is what she called it. She had been ready to get back on a horse weeks ago but everybody had told her they would break her good leg if she did.

Her shoulder was pretty much as good as new with only some pain when she lifted things. Her leg of course still bothered her a lot but the doctors assured her it would take some time to heal. She still had to hobble around on those detestable crutches.

With Hank being dead, she was a widow. She and Justin set a date for early fall to get married. Jesse was so glad Justin finally realized how much he needed her.

Two weeks after getting out of the hospital, Jesse got a major shock. A check came in the mail for Hank's life insurance claim of one million dollars. She had called Hailey but she informed Jesse there was no mistake and that it was her money free and clear.

"Hey sleepyhead, are you awake?" Justin called from the hallway.

"Yes I am, come in."

"I brought you breakfast." He placed a tray full of bacon and eggs on the nightstand.

"You're going to get me fat."

"We'll work it off you tonight," Justin teased.

Ignoring his remark she quickly turned the subject her way. "Hey, how are the men doing in the cave?" She had hired a group of miners to thoroughly comb the cavern and look for gold or any other items of interest. They had come up so far with two other skeletons that the coroner was trying to identify.

Hank, Charlie, Gus, and Annie were buried in Republic. The whole community came to see they were put to rest for what they had done. Jesse made sure the big bay gelding had a spot in the barn to call home. He turned out to be a great horse, or so Justin had told her; she knew she would have to find out for herself once she could ride again. Maybe she would claim him as her new gelding. She hadn't made up her mind yet.

"Well, that's what I really came to talk to you about, Jess." Justin had been up on the mountain helping the miners in their search for almost a month now and he had seen very little gold taken out.

"What is it?" Jesse knew this conversation was going to happen sooner rather than later. She had heard that they hadn't found much.

"I think we should call it quits on the mining. Old Henry hid his gold better than anything we're using can detect," Justin explained.

"So you think there's no gold?" Jesse asked.

"I didn't say that. I just think we have spent enough time looking for something that should remain hidden."

"Saddle Monty for me. I want to go to the cave."

"Can't I just drive you up? We cut a road right to the cave entrance."

Jesse smiled; she had forgotten about that. "Okay, I guess you can drive me there."

Justin picked Jesse up and carried her down the stairs and out to the truck. They drove the short distance up to the cave entrance. Once out front, Justin stopped the truck and came around to Jesse's door to help her out.

"No, Justin, I want to walk this on my own." Jesse sounded determined and Justin realized this was something she was going to do on her own.

"At least hold my hand."

"That I can manage." They walked down the well lit tunnel and came out into the open part of the cavern where Jesse cringed at the thought of the last time she had been there and all the pain and suffering she had gone through with those bullets. She looked towards the tunnel Hank had been found in.

Justin felt her tense beside him. "You okay?"

"Yes, of course." She wasn't, but her pride wouldn't let her tell him that her leg hurt like the dickens and this place creeped her out to no end.

"You sure?" Justin asked again.

"Yes, honey, I'm sure. I was just thinking that I wish I hadn't killed Gus and Annie so we could know why they did all this to us."

"I know what you mean. An explanation would be nice."

"Why did they kill? They ended up with quite a list of murders: Hank, Cozy, Jack, Bill, and Jinks. I just wish I knew why."

"If I had to guess I would say maybe Annie and Hank had brainstormed the whole thing with help from Charlie, and then Annie betrayed Hank for Gus, and that's when they killed Hank. But I'm thinking that Charlie and Gus did most of the killing. I'll bet Jack was killed before Gus came into the picture. Otherwise I couldn't imagine him letting Charlie kill Jack. At least that was what the police thought happened."

"And what about Cozy and Jinks? What about Bill?"

"I think they were all killed to get to us, in a manner of speaking."

"I guess that sounds like as good of an explanation as any." Jesse started as a loud scream filled the air around her. She practically jumped right into Justin's arms.

"What was that!"

"I'm not sure. Hey guys, it's Justin, where are you?"

"Justin! We're down here! Tunnel six, come quick!" a voice answered back. Justin knew it was Harry, one of the main bosses of the miners.

"Come on, Jesse." Justin ushered her as he headed down tunnel six until they ran almost smack into Harry, who was sitting in the tunnel looking confused next to a pile of dirt that had come down off the side of the tunnel.

"Oh my gosh, Harry, are you okay? Did the cavern cave in on you?"

Harry looked up into Justin and Jesse's worried faces, his face covered in dirt and streaked with mud.

"I found it. I found it!" He jumped up and started dancing a jig in the tunnel at the small entrance that he had dug away to reveal a small cavern with old sacks piled to the ceiling.

"You found it. Henry's gold! Oh my gosh, we're rich!"

Jesse screamed as she jumped on one leg with Harry, Justin, and a couple of the other miners who ran to them when they heard the news.

Justin pulled Jesse into his arms and hugged her close to him for a long time before he spoke.

"We found it, Jesse," he whispered into her ear.

"Yes we did. We found what almost got us killed, what Hank, Annie, Charlie, and Gus spent days or weeks looking for. We found it."

"You're a rich woman."

"And you're a rich man."

"You still want to marry me?" Justin inquired.

"Yes." She softly pressed her lips to his in a sweet and meaningful kiss that was meant to say forever. She reluctantly pulled away and looked into his blue eyes. "You still want to marry me, Justin?"

"Of course, Jesse, I love you. No matter who is trying to kill you." He smiled as he kissed her nose.

"I love you too."

"Then I think we were rich long before we found this gold." They stood and looked out over the many bags of Old Henry's gold that filled the cavern.

"I can't believe the legend was true, Jess."

"I find that hilarious."

"Why's that?"

"Because you and I were the only ones who didn't believe in the legend."

"When you put it that way, it is kind of funny."

"But Justin, you and I also didn't believe in love, and just look at us now." Jesse smiled up into Justin's tanned features. She loved him, and for the first time in her life she knew what it was like to be loved completely for who she was.

Justin smiled as he leaned in close for another kiss.

"Yes. Just look at us now."

The End

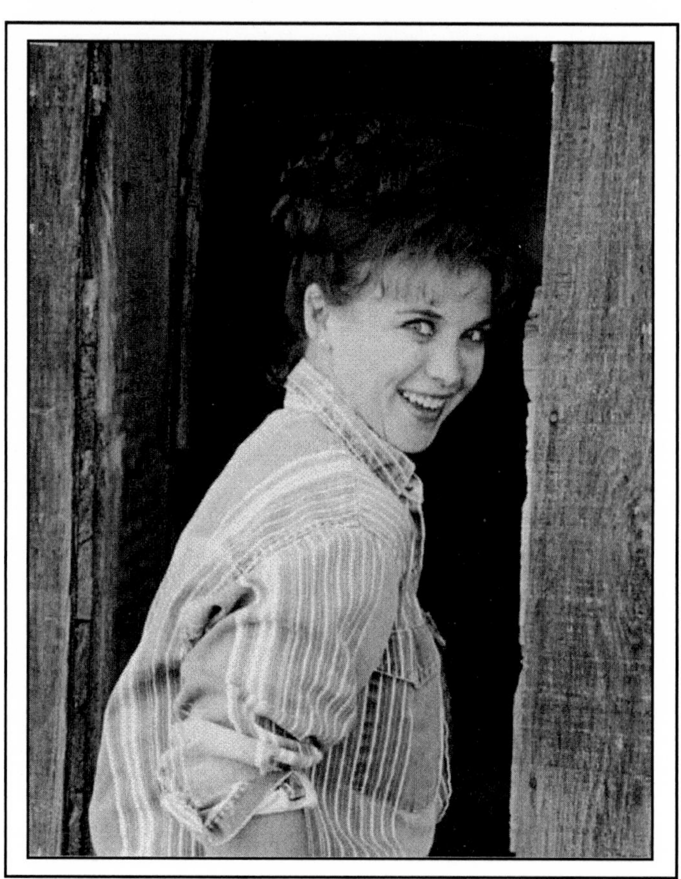

About the Author

Dawn Nelson is a true cowgirl. She was born and raised on a cattle ranch in northeastern Washington state. Married to a cattle rancher, she now calls Creston, Washington, her home.

Dawn, her husband Kris, and their daughter Laren own and operate a large cattle ranch in central Washington. Dawn enjoys showing her registered cattle, riding horses, camping, hunting, and other outdoor activities. She also volunteers a lot of her time to 4-H and is actively involved in her county Cattlemen's Association.

Her previous work includes A Cowgirl Remembers When (2009), The Colt (2010), and A Cowgirl Never Forgets (2010), all from Gray Dog Press, Spokane, Washington.